To Janet

Enjoy reading chaos.

Donna   x

Keep chaosing !

ANNA McKANN's

CHAVOS

The Kids of Distrito Federal

Sharon House Publishing

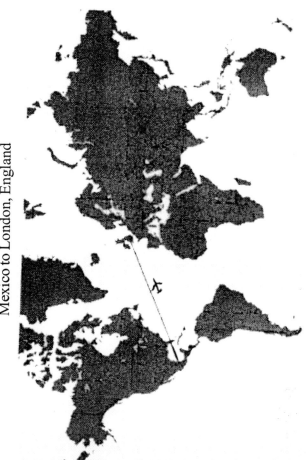

World map showing the flight from
Mexico to London, England

It is 5,557 miles from Heathrow to Mexico City

Map of the Mexican Metro system

CHAVOS
THE KIDS OF DISTRITO FEDERAL

First published in 2006
by Sharon House Publishing Ltd
Sharon House, 152 Wakefield Road,
Ossett, West Yorkshire WF5 9AQ

Printed in England by Write Books

ISBN 0-9554438-0-6
978-0-9554438-0-0

"Whilst this book has been written, based on many real life situations and true incidents, the characters are actually fictitious and any resemblance to a certain individual must be taken as pure coincidence."

ACKNOWLEDGMENTS/ AGRADECIMIENTOS

i would like to express my deepest thanks and warmest regards to all who have made this book possible. Most especially to Catherine and Julie and the staff at Rainbow Childcare who have lovingly taken care of my kindergartens during my overseas visits.

A huge thanks to all those institutions and Children's Homes in Mexico City who allowed me to visit their premises. Much gratitude to the Street Crisis Teams who allowed me to accompany them. In particular, thanks to the workers at *Casa Alianza*.

Tons of love to the volunteers at Sedac and those very special Mexican ladies who treated me as a sister, although I was a *güera*. Most particularly Sari who has been no less than an angel; without her this book would never have been possible.

Love and stuff to my family and my wonderful children. Natalie, who accepted my constant disappearance overseas without complaining, although she missed me so! And Tim, who has been a wonderful source of inspiration and encouragement.

A big thank you to my adorable Spanish tutor for her patience and friendship and to my dentist... thereby lies another story!

Finally, thanks to the Street Kids for their openness, honesty and for sharing with me.

All that's left to say is: I pray this book, the first of many, will become a huge success and I hereby donate all the profits from the sale to making our world a better place for the kids.

Love to children everywhere,

Anna

ALL PROCEEDS FROM THIS BOOK WILL GO TO R.C.C. INTERNATIONAL CHARITY REG NO: 1100038

www.rccinternational.org.uk

Intriguing..... An emotional read......

Compelling.... An action-packed story,
full of intrigue & suspense.

Utterly believable.....makes page-turning
unavoidable.

An absorbing read.... A must-have for all young readers.

A brilliant first novel....

A most impressive debut about friendship,
courage & culture.

Miss H Stocks
Deputy Head, Cliff School

An emotional and educational story, I loved it!

I would love to read the sequel, it was fantastic!

I enjoyed reading it! Just wanted to read, read, read.

10/10 It was fantastic!

Comments from children at Cliff School,
aged 9-10

Written beautifully, imaginative
but based on truth.
Can't wait to read the sequel.
A book every kid should read. Certain to be a movie.

Irma Alicia Fassioli Manrique
Consul General del Peru

Had me enthralled from beginning to end...
Could not put it down, excellent book for both adults and
children to learn of the lives of these street kids.

This could be the start of something big.....

Charlotte Agnew
Write Books

ABOUT THE AUTHOR

A nna McKann was born in Yorkshire, England
and cares not to give her age, "You are as old as
you feel," she says, "and I feel like a teenager at the
moment – as though my life has just begun."

Indeed, Anna's life took an amazing turn about ten
years ago when, as a committed Christian, she prayed
that God would give real purpose to her life. In
September 2003, she booked a flight to Mexico City
with no itinerary, plans or pre-arrangements, she went
adlib.

"I don't have an adventurous spirit and I'm not brave,"
said Anna, "but I just knew I had to go to Mexico. What
I saw there, lived and breathed, touched my heart and
gave me inspiration for my first novel."

Hence, the story of the Street Kids begins…

CHAPTERS   PAGE

PRELUDE

Dolita

Raggy Man

A bandoned as a baby but taken under the wing of a beggar woman named Old Ma Kensie, Dolita's life has been anything but easy. At the age of five, she joined a group of homeless kids, living behind the metro in Mexico D.F., hidden in a makeshift shelter.

Life on the streets brings pain, suffering and trauma, but Dolita finds comfort in friendship, triumph and her dreams.

Together with her scruffy companion and best friend, Raggy Man, her guts and his faithfulness enable them to embark on adventure after adventure, where there's no room for mistakes and survival's the game...

CHAPTER 1
THE COFFEE SHOP

The first week had passed slowly and Charlotte glanced at the dregs in the empty ceramic pot. Her eyes focused upon the well-used journal and dog-eared notepad on the table beside her.

The journal read:

Day 7. 10th September
"Feeling homesick! Another wretched headache! Obviously not acclimatised yet: high altitude and poor air quality! Desperately missing home."

Written with a scratchy pen were the words:

"Why am I here? Crazy or what?!"

Charlotte tried to ignore the group of nauseating men at the table beside her who were so desperately irritating. Why did they have to talk so loudly? She was sure no one else was interested in their business, and she certainly was not! Contemplating telling them to quieten down she stood up to get a refill of the scrumptious frothy coffee, thinking she also rather fancied a cheese and ham panini. They did look good and the ache in her belly reminded her she had not taken lunch. Suddenly, startled by a face peering in through the window, her eyes were transfixed by his. It was an eerie feeling and for a few moments she couldn't help but stare. It took her a while to realise what it was that unsettled her. His face was cute but something was very disturbing. His eyes, yes those large dark eyes! Just two quite enormous black pupils staring through the window at her, and then suddenly he was gone. He was pulled aside by another older-looking kid. Charlotte shuddered. Trying to dismiss the image, she ordered her coffee. Forgetting the panini she returned to her seat, relieved that the group of boisterous, loud-mouthed men were gathering up their belongings to leave.

Her back to the window, pen in hand, she began writing in her journal:

"This is hard, probably one of the hardest things I have ever done in my whole life, but I am here for a purpose..."

She paused.

Someone turned up the music and she felt a little less homesick. It was a good old English song and one of her grandmother's favourites – *Qué será, será*. Whatever will be, will be. The future's not ours to see. *Qué será, será*. She did not hear the commotion outside a little later and continued writing.

* * *

"Get these street kids out of here!" shouted the burly security guard angrily, as the limousine began to approach. "They make the place look untidy," he grunted. "*¡Cochinos!* Gives us a bad impression! Come on, move them on. *¡Rápido!*" His gestures were aggressive, his eyes cold and lacking compassion. He lurched forwards to push one of the kids who quickly dodged out of his reach.

"Move, *escuincla!*" he screeched. Not a very endearing term, but one often used by the guards. The kids, about seven of them in all, were passing by and had stopped for a few moments to catch their breath. One of them, a little one who had been trailing behind, adjusted her shoes, which were ill-fitting and cutting deeply into her heels. The little girl's feet were full of weeping sores and were badly swollen. Two more steps and she came to the realisation that no shoes was better than badly fitting ones!

She discarded them, intending to continue her journey barefoot. One of the hotel security guys picked up the shoes, grimacing as though he were holding some sort of alien being that had just crawled up from the gutter. He proceeded to sling them into the nearest trash-can, careful to hold them by his fingertips, at a distance from his body. The kids moved on, the little one still trailing behind, a pained expression on her troubled face.

She was a pretty little thing with olive skin, a mass of thick brown, raggy hair, matted and uncombed. She had big brown eyes like saucers. Her brown linen dress was tatty and torn, resting just above her knees, revealing them to be grazed and sore. Over her shoulder hung a dirty plastic bag, the contents of which one dare not imagine! She stopped the far side of a clump of bushes and peered through, brushing aside the evergreen leaves and the tiny white sparkle-like flowers.

The aroma from the bush had a powerful honey
scent, enough to stop anyone in their tracks. Being

careful to move away from a rather large obnoxious
looking bee, which had been attracted by the aroma,
she watched the entrance of the rather grand and
elaborate hotel. Just at that moment a limousine
pulled to a halt outside the large welcoming doors.
The limo's long sleek white body, black leather top
and tinted windows looked superb.

A rather dashing, well-dressed chauffeur exited,
and another equally handsome guy jumped out of
the passenger side. He opened the rear doors to reveal
a flamboyant, skinny, middle-aged woman, wearing
a mauve, silk dress that cascaded over her bony hips.
A younger, rounded and shorter, less well-dressed
woman sat beside her, and a girl of a similar stature
and age to the street kid. As if there were some great
urgency the men quickly escorted the women and
the girl into the hotel foyer, leaving the rear door of
the limo temporarily ajar.

Glancing quickly towards the open door, a flicker of light from within revealed a light-cream interior, cherry-coloured wood and a mirrored ceiling. The limousine also boasted a drinks bar and a flat screen television (which the kid would have seen had she been able to glimpse inside a little further).

Luxury or what?!

The street kid paid little attention to the women. Suffice to say they were both relatively well dressed. Now the girl, that was a different matter! Peering at her inquisitively, she noticed that she wore a black embroidered, velvet jacket with gold embossed cuffs, double lapels and brass shiny buttons, a short black skirt and knee-high red suede boots. Swinging a red bag, preferring to wear one red glove and carry the other, she looked haughty and self-opinionated.

Under her arm she carried a tiny dog, the tiniest dog the kid had ever seen. The little dog was adorned with a red bow in its hair, which matched the girl's boots and gloves perfectly. To make it look even worse it had a red plaited lead and some sort of red feathery thing around its neck. It had a cute but very pointy face, bulging eyes and a big black nose that looked too large for its face. It truly was a comical sight. The kid watched bemused as the two of them disappeared into the hotel foyer.

A gold trolley was wheeled out and several suitcases and bags were unloaded from the boot of the limo.

Each piece of luggage was placed systematically on the trolley. The cases all matched perfectly. Fuchsia pink!

"Yuk!" she thought, and before she could see another thing one of the older boys ran back for her. He scooped her up in his arms, scolding her.

"¡Dolita, Dolita!" he said. "Don't lag behind."

"¡*Tengo hambre!*" she whimpered

"Well then, we'll try and find you some food!" And off they went.

The limousine engine started and its sleek body slowly passed them by. It could be seen disappearing in the same direction from which it came.

Street kids were rarely seen in this part of the city. Perhaps occasionally when passing through they would stop outside the famous coffee shop adjacent to the hotel. (Not to go in; that would never do!) They would hover outside expectantly. Well occasionally someone pressed a coin into their grubby hands, but for the most part they were ignored. Ignored? Oh yes, but not by everyone (though it seemed that way sometimes!) They were treated like outcasts, a nuisance, an embarrassment to society. Yet there were those who gave every waking hour to helping them. Those with a passion in their hearts, those who had become the friends of the street kids; and this is where my story begins - in the streets of downtown Mexico City.

"Street kids," I hear you say. "Who are they? What are they?" Well, maybe you don't have a street kid problem where you live. But believe me, there is such a problem in the world today. Hang on in there. Keep reading and you will find out just who the street kids or '*chavos*' really are!

CHAPTER 2
DOLITA

My story begins eight years ago with a girl called Taiawah and the child that she abandoned on the streets; the child that you will come to know and love as much as I do.

Who am I, do you say? Oh me, I am just the storyteller, but the child is Dolita.

Taiawah was only 17 years old when Dolita was born, but first of all allow me to tell you a little about Taiawah and her life. As you may guess by her name, she was of Indian origin. Her several-times-great grandfather had once been chief of a very grand Indian tribe and Taiawah loved to listen to the stories of years gone by. She would often sit as a little girl on her grandfather's knee and listen to the wise old man as he shared stories about the heroes of the past. Taiawah did not know how old her grandfather was, but his white hair and brown, wrinkled, pitted skin, made her think he was at least 110! Once a man of great stature, strength and sagacity, now struggling to walk, he limped with the help of a beautifully carved stick, insisting always on wearing his brown suede waistcoat, knee-high boots and hat. He never went anywhere without his infamous hat. The hat with the bright red feather that is! He had even been known to sleep in it. How could anyone sleep in a hat? Really!

Dark Eyes, as he was called, could often be found sitting under the tree by the stream, at the far side of the piece of land that her family once owned. Taiawah would, as a little girl, run over to him gleefully and ask him to tell her a story. Some of the other children also loved to gather round to listen to his stories.

Taiawah always felt special and she knew that she was undoubtedly the "apple of his eye." She was the one who would sit closest at his feet and, when allowed, sit on his knee. His eyes were truly dark and Taiawah often saw a great sadness within them. She remembered that her grandfather said… "The eyes are the windows to the soul and you can tell much about a person's heart from looking into their eyes."

Taiawah did not have a father; at least she had never known him. She was told that he had gone away before she was born. She never dared mention him again, remembering the time when her mother became very angry with her, sternly saying, "We can manage quite well without him thank you very much, and don't bring up the subject again!"

Maybe one reason why she was particularly fond of her old grandfather was because he was the only man in her life, and especially the only person who showed her any kindness or real love.

Taiawah was the youngest of four children, the others being boys, now gone away. Instead of looking after her they had usually teased and bullied her. She had a hard life but, for the most part, she was a happy, contented little girl. Taiawah could not read or write but she was very skilled with her hands. From an early age her mother had taught her the skills for which her ancestors were renowned, the skills of basketry and fine art. She loved to paint the orange pottery once the elders of her community had fashioned and shaped it. Most of all she had taken great pride in painting the tiny beads and then threading them together to make the exquisite and most beautiful jewellery which they later sold at the markets.

As the years passed Taiawah grew into a beautiful, delicate young woman. She was no longer the little

girl that used to sit on her grandfather's knee. Her legs were long and slender, her skin bronzed, her complexion fresh.

When brushed, Taiawah's chestnut coloured hair was so long she could even sit on it. Occasionally she would be seen to wash it in the stream; a mixture of crushed banana, oil from the eucalyptus plant and coconut maintained its excellent sheen. The younger children would often call out,

"Show us you hair Taiawah. Can you sit on it Taiawah?"

Preferring to wear it in two pigtails, she braided and plaited it with thin strips of interwoven ribbon and some of the brightly coloured beads that she had proudly painted herself. Taiawah was truly becoming very beautiful but, as she grew older, so did her grandfather.

Dark Eyes was very quiet and withdrawn on one particular morning. Taiawah had noticed that his health had been failing for some time. She loved her grandfather with all her heart. Her older brothers had grown up and moved away and she rarely saw her mother since she had met a man in the village and spent most of her days cooking and cleaning for him. A lazy man who rarely worked, he spent many hours each day sleeping off a drunken stupor. Taiawah hated him for taking her mother away. "Bewitched her," she would say. How foolish her mother was! Taiawah realised that was in fact the very thing she had done this past few months for her grandfather; cooking, cleaning, fetching and carrying. Of course, that was different. Quite different! He was old and needed someone to take care of him. She loved to take care of him; whatever would she do if something happened to him? He had become her life. Everything she did revolved around the beloved old man.

"Taiawah," he called. "Walk with me by the stream and then come sit with me. Perhaps later, granddaughter, you will make your old grandfather some of the scrumptious beef broth that you make so well. Plenty of spices!" he added.

"Sure I will," she said, reaching for his old, twisted hickory walking stick and a cosy blanket to drape over his shoulders.

"It's early grandfather and the sun is not yet out. You must keep warm." And as she looked into his eyes she saw a sparkle, something different to that which she had ever seen before. She knew in her spirit, today was no ordinary day. Today was going to be different. What happened next she had not quite expected however. At least not so soon, without a period of warning. Today her life was going to change forever.

Sitting with her grandfather under the foliage of the enormous juniper tree, which overshadowed the stream, they chatted like two young school friends. She watched him as he brushed aside a cluster of the bluish-green, needle-like leaves that had fallen from the tree. He broke open one of the dark-blue cones revealing several small berry-like seeds. Turning his attention to the mature tree he took his small pocket knife and began to scrape at the durable wood releasing its fragrance. An oily substance oozed out, which she knew to have great medicinal benefits, excellent for various skin diseases. They talked endlessly, seemingly for hours. Longer than they had ever talked before! Dark Eyes told her about her grandmother and how special their relationship had been. How she loved horses and, sadly, the great passion of her life had been her downfall. Her adventurous spirit when riding too fast led her to try to jump a boulder. Thrown from the horse, she was sadly killed by a severe blow to the head. "Taiawah," he whispered, "looking at you is such a blessing. You are so like your grandmother in looks and mannerisms. You even have the same mischievous laugh!"

Then he told her the story he most loved to tell about his people. "The Cloud People," so called because they had once lived high in the northern territory, so high in the mountains that often the clouds would hang on the mountain top making them invisible to the rest of the world. The cloud forests were a hunting ground for his family, but as time passed a shortage of food forced them to leave the land they so loved and descend the mountains and settle in the villages. Many had settled in the Valley of Oaxaca. The great tribe of Mixtec Indians and others like them began to scatter.

"Oooh, tell me more about them grandfather. The Mixtecs did you say?"

"Yes," he replied, "and they were hard workers, no doubt about that. They undertook many commercial ventures: trouble is they had one downfall."

"What's that grandfather?"

"Alcohol."

"Oh. Go on, why haven't you told me all this before?"

His story continued, as he spoke of his own grandfather "White Eagle," the great and mighty warrior. Also of the famous Spanish conquistador, Cortés, who took eventual possession of much of the land, introducing the new language of Spanish to the communities. As the Indians retained their own native language, so the Spanish and Indians began to live together. He told her how, before the Spanish arrived, many of the plants in Oaxaca did not exist. The settlers brought many fruits, flowers, trees and vegetables, including the radish. Taiawah laughed because her grandfather loved radishes.

"As it happened, one year the crop of radishes was so abundant that a section was not harvested and lay dormant for months. Then one day, two of the Spanish friars uprooted some of the forgotten radishes and were both amazed and amused to see the size and shapes. The huge misshapen roots began to attract the crowds wherever they were sold."

She listened with intrigue as he continued.

"They were soon being shaped and carved into figures. Each year thereafter the radishes were shaped and moulded into characters from Nativity scenes. A contest for the best nativity scene and characters evolved. That is why you will see the celebrations on December 23rd each year and the Festival of the Radishes has become a night to remember in Oaxaca to this day."

"Wow!" she said, her face beaming with interest.

Dark Eyes then told Taiawah about the many gods that his people had worshiped. The rain god, the sun god, the moon god, "… in fact they had a god for everything!" he exclaimed. He then told her about the God that Cortés spoke of, the Christian God. As his memories unfolded like the reading of a history book, so his voice began to waver.

"You are weak grandfather," she exclaimed "and you are shivering. We must go back to the house at once. I will bring you the hot beef broth that you so love."

Looking into his eyes she would remember his next words forever.

"To everything there is a season my girl, a time for every purpose under heaven. A time to be born and a time to die. A time to plant and a time to pluck, a time to dance and to mourn." His eyes looked deep into hers as if he were speaking into her very being.

"Your life here is over my child. You have dreams eh?"

"Yes of course grandfather; you know my dream is to go to the city," she whispered with a slight tremor in her voice.

"You are a young woman now with a life of your own. Go! And may God be with you."

He closed his eyes and went to sleep in his favourite place by the cool waters of the stream in the shade of the great juniper tree.

She never did get him back to the house to enjoy his last bowl of beef broth. He died that day and some of the locals took care of the burial. Wrapped in a rich multi-coloured blanket, his favourite clothes, including his hat, his walking stick and his old hunting gear by his side. His face painted and his hair plaited he looked the ever-famous warrior he once was. Her face no longer bright with joy, she felt a sense of total despair.

Taiawah looked upon him for the last time and thought her heart was breaking.

* * *

Three months passed and Taiawah had left Oaxaca with a few precious belongings – a few spare clothes, items of jewellery, which she hoped to sell, and some sentimental things that her grandfather had given her. She had also packed fruit, nuts and pulses. She took as many bananas as she could carry, knowing they, along with the nuts, were a great source of energy and would sustain her for a while. Taking one of her grandfather's hand-woven favourite blankets, she rolled it and tied it carefully over the top of her rucksack before leaving.

Making her way to the great city, a journey that once would have taken many hours, was now considerably shorter with the new freeway.

Taiawah had a little money, sufficient for the *autobus* fare and to last a couple of weeks, three if she was careful. She was so certain that she would find work, maybe as a housekeeper or maid in one of the grand houses? Whatever, it was time to move on, of that she was sure. There was little work and no future for her now in Oaxaca. Unfortunately for Taiawah it seemed that everyone else had decided to go to the city too and she soon realised finding work was no easy task.

Indeed, until the money ran out the city was everything she had ever hoped for. She felt it as soon as she arrived. The colour, diversity and liveliness seemed to flow endlessly: beautiful buildings, art galleries and monuments. The Angel, oh yes the beautiful golden statue of the Angel on the Paseo de la Reforma, the city's main boulevard, was breathtaking. The Reforma, one of the city's status addresses, stretched southward, connecting new elegant constructions, offices, hotels and banks, with the oldest section of the city. There she found cobblestone alleys and small *plazas*. The city was alive and Taiawah soon had no need of her meager food supply, for it was during one of those lively evenings that she met him - the man of her dreams and, as her resources were now exhausted, he provided for her every need. At least in the beginning. Unfortunately, since that fatal meeting things had not worked out as she had planned. In fact everything had gone so miserably wrong. She had made some bad decisions, oh yes, no doubt about that but, after all, she was young. Some would say immature: not yet 17, she lacked wisdom.

With all the bitterness and resentment in her heart from the loss of her beloved grandfather and the rejection felt by the abandonment of her mother, the loneliness that she now began to find in the big city compounded her grief. Strange, she thought, how one could be so lonely amongst so many people. She sank deeper and deeper into depression. The most gorgeous-looking guy had caught her eye and she latched onto him. In no time at all, she became his woman. She fell for his charm and he fell for her beauty.

"*¡Qué mango!*" exclaimed one of the young *chicas*, when he walked into the bar.

"What's that supposed to mean?" asked Taiawah. "Delicious," replied the girl.

Well delicious he was and he was soon deliciously hers. His name was Juan Carlos and he was indeed very handsome! A Spaniard by birth, his family originated from the Spanish capital of Madrid. Unfortunately he was a thief and a liar. She soon became pregnant with their first baby, he was on his way to prison and Taiawah was now more alone than ever!

So the story of Dolita begins, in downtown Mexico City, otherwise known as *Distrito Federal*.

Dolita was born 14th of April at 3.15 in the afternoon. A spring baby and a most beautiful one too. With big brown eyes and tiny fingers and toes, the little miracle of life that was all too often taken for granted. Taiawah wondered what her own father was like and how her heart ached as she thought of the father Dolita may never know.

Juan Carlos, Dolita's father, was much older than Taiawah. At first she had felt safe, as he had instantly taken her under his protection. He had lived about forty minutes drive out of the city centre in the area known as Xochmilco. There his home had been a small, single-room *casita* at the side of one of the canals and his days were often spent in the tiny timber yard adjacent. She had stayed with him for several weeks and soon after Juan Carlos was arrested, having found out that she was pregnant, she felt her best option was to return to the city centre and find work. Taiawah never did find out exactly what he was into but she soon realised he had lots of unsavoury friends. The police had found quite a stash of narcotics in the timber yard when they took him away. Taiawah thought then that she was better without him and never did try to locate his whereabouts.

Subsequently, Taiawah survived and was very grateful for the help that she received from the Mexican family who employed her to help in their small bakery; homemade cakes, fresh loaves, sweet bread and all manner of culinary delights, not to mention scrumptious cookies, were available daily. She loved her time helping in the kitchen, in spite of the fact that she could not enjoy the many cookies herself, as the first four months of her pregnancy were spent in a state of perpetual nausea.

The family were most kind and benevolent and allowed her to stay in their home for a little while before and after the birth of the baby.

There came a time however when grumpy old granny came to stay and then the trouble began. They were overcrowded. Granny was an absolute walking nightmare and when Dolita was a few weeks old it was time for Taiawah to move out.

Having found this place she looked around with such sadness in her spirit. At least in Oaxaca she had some of the niceties of life. How did she go so miserably wrong? Her grandfather's words whirled round and round in her head.

"Go to the city, follow your dreams." This was not the dream that she had imagined and she yearned to be back in her old homestead. To sit by the stream under that oh so familiar Juniper tree! To hear the birds singing and the sound of the running water as it tumbled over the rocks and rippled down stream. How she longed for that sweet smell of the Oaxaca Valley once again, where she remembered the fresh scent of the forest immediately after the rain had fallen and the odour of the sweet tree sap on a warm day.

She would even be pleased to see one of the familiar grey squirrels, even though she had learnt to hate them as a child because one had savagely bitten her little finger. In contrast, outside she could hear the continuous noise of the traffic and then, suddenly, a thud followed by raised and angry voices. She heard the high-pitched piercing siren of the local *policia* in the distance and the angry raised voices of drunkards being thrown out of the tiny alehouse, two blocks down. The cantina as it was called, was a rowdy drinking place. Full of men, it boasted a raucous atmosphere and tonight was no exception. The neon lights from the 24-hour store lit up her room as they flashed intermittently.

She cradled the young Dolita in her arms and together they fell asleep, Taiawah thinking of the future, and what would become of them, with no money, living in the old downtown shack that had become their home.

(HAPTER 3
EIGHT YEARS LATER

D olita was awake very early. She had been deliciously lost in her dreams. You see the young Dolita was quite a dreamer and was naturally disgruntled, annoyed at being disturbed. What a blow she thought. Her dreams, which were becoming more common, gave her some respite from the drudgery and misery of the streets.

Throwing the dirty infested blanket aside, now wide-awake, her eyes felt gritty and sore. Something had jolted her awake yet all was quiet and still in the shelter apart from a few soft whistles and gentle snores. Strange! She pulled the tatty grey blanket over her head and snuggled down once again. A few moments later and, feeling quite restless, Dolita peered over the top of the blanket, "Blast!" she said, unable to go back to sleep.

"How irritating!" There it was again, thunderous noise! She wondered how the others could possibly sleep through that racket, realising it was the hurry and bustle of the market traders setting up for the day on the *Calle Micalo* below. Why oh why did they have to start so early? Everyone else in the shelter slept on, oblivious to the noises of the outside world.

Dolita then heard shouting. What a commotion! She recognised the voice to be undoubtedly that of Papa Joe. He sounded very angry. Joe was from

Colombia, an extrovert, flamboyant personality. Then, many Latinos were.

When he was passionate about something, he was truly passionate. When he was angry, he was painfully angry! At such times the most sensible option anyone could take was to keep well out of his way. Papa Joe would not think twice about giving you a clip around the ear, if you came within ear shot that is! He had a critical spirit and no one could do anything right for him. You know the sort - do a thing well and it goes unnoticed; do one thing wrong and he makes a real song and dance about it. Dolita could not imagine what it was like living with the grumpy old codger. He only had one arm and no one dare ask what happened to the other. Perhaps that was why he was so unpleasant, bad memories, trauma, and all that stuff.

Dolita crept out of the shelter slipping and sliding down the muddy banking into the street below, unnoticed by the others who slept on. She peered round the back of Papa Joe's old rusty transit van to see what was happening. Waving his one good arm around, he was grumbling and complaining at Rosa, who was busy setting up her stall beside his. The barrow boy came round the corner just at that precise moment and, by the look on his face and his body language, wished he hadn't. His barrow was full to the brim with succulent green asparagus, which he sold on the move as he meandered between the other traders.

"Get out of the way!" shouted Papa Joe, nearly colliding with the barrow and pushing the boy angrily out of his path. Dolita's eyes then fixed on the pathway adjacent to Papa Joe and there were eggs everywhere. Yes eggs, all over the place and what a mess too. Hardboiled eggs, so I suppose it could have been worse she thought, raising her hand to her mouth to cover the gasp. Imagine, had they not been hard-boiled, yuk! No wonder Papa Joe was angry. Mrs Joe would have spent all the previous night boiling them for Papa Joe to sell on his stall the next day. Lovely with salt and dips, they went down a treat. Even the local *policía* had been known to stop and buy a salted egg with their favourite dip.

Dolita was sad, but at the same time could not help being just a little amused. Papa Joe was so funny when he was angry, scary but funny. He had an exceptionally long ponytail, neatly tied back with a piece of decadent white lace. His hair was now particularly grey and he boasted a beard and a moustache that had a mind of its own, curling at the edges. The moustache that is not the beard! Dolita had never seen anyone quite like him and when he was angry the moustache seemed to curl all the more. Unable to contain her amusement any longer and trying not to laugh out loud she squealed like a baby pig. Papa Joe, seeing her, stomped towards her, he was absolutely furious, his face now dark with rage. How dare anyone laugh at his misfortune and a scruffy little *escuincla* at that too! Dolita, sensing she had to move fast, dodged as Joe lunged forward to grab her by her hair but she was gone. No one could move like Dolita. She was out of there, and she intended to avoid him for quite some time too.

Dolita was now over 8 years old. "Eight years going on 18 more like," said Rosa. "How come you know so much?"

"Just do!" replied Dolita, grinning and chuckling as she sped off with the piece of palatable soft cheese that Rosa had given her, making sure that Papa Joe was nowhere to be seen after the egg incident. Well of course he had picked up most of the eggs, discarding them in an old rusty trash-can standing conveniently nearby. He had left the rest in disgust and gone home. No eggs, no money. She certainly would not want to be around when he told Mrs Papa Joe!

Dolita liked Rosa. She was a "real gypsy," Romany they say! You know, the sort who lived in one of those fabulous caravans, the rounded ones pulled by horses. A "Diovado" so called, ornately painted in a brilliant red, black and shimmering gold. It really was a sight for sore eyes. From Rosa's description it appears that in such a small space there was absolutely everything that one could possibly need and more! A collector she was, trinkets and ornaments filled every nook and cranny. Rosa had her own language and when she broke out into the Romany gypsy twang, the other traders didn't have the slightest clue what she was talking about. She told fascinating tales of her travelling days and interesting as they were, sadly she knew her roaming days were over.

"I suspect she was very beautiful as a young gypsy girl," thought Dolita. She had such a pretty face but as for her stature, she was now as round as she was tall.

"Too much cheese I think," said one of the street kids. "Her stomach is so big she can't see her toes!

She sells a piece, eats a piece. Just watch her. She's beginning to look like a piece of cheese!"

True enough Rosa was always eating, but how could anyone look like a piece of cheese? Honestly! Dolita puzzled.

Rosa had thick black hair wrapped around like a bird's nest on the top of her head. She always wore huge earrings and a large number of bangles and beads. Some of the kids were cheeky to Rosa but they all loved her really. I suppose one has to say there was also a little rivalry, perhaps even jealousy, between them because you see, Dolita was her favourite. Come to think of it, Dolita was everyone's favourite. Just 'cos she was a girl and cute? No, I don't think so; more than that. There was something very  special about young Dolita and everyone knew it. Undoubtedly, she was the sweetest person on the streets. If she had it she would share it. Of course, there was the "Street Kid Code" but unfortunately not everyone obeyed the code.

"Code! Rules! No such thing as rules on the street," said Mikey Mean who never shared anything.

"If we are to survive we look after one another!" insisted Enrique, the oldest in the group.

"Rubbish, look after yourself I say," said Mikey. "Rules. Forget the rules!" Hence, he acquired the nickname "Mikey Mean." Yes, as you might expect, no one liked him.

Oops, before I go any further I had better introduce you to "The Street Kid Gang" and, I suppose, you want to know how Dolita became part of the gang. Well it's a simple story really and it all began with the old beggar woman named Kensie, the one later called Ma Kensie 'cos she was like a grandmother to them all.

Old Ma Kensie had lived on the streets most of her life. No one knew how old she was but Dolita thought she looked at least 110. Well, perhaps not quite so old, but very old! She could be found walking the streets by day and huddled up in shop doorways at night. Her favourite spot was the *Oficina de Ventas* at the corner of the flower market.

 There she made her home, which consisted of two plastic carrier bags full of all her worldly belongings and a woven multicoloured blanket, which she carried on her back, tied and rolled with a piece of yellow string. Ma Kensie wore an old ankle-length black woollen dress, and flat black shoes displaying holes at the front where her dirty toes protruded. She wore a red tatty cardigan and she usually had a

grubby black hand-crochet shawl draped around her shoulders. Boasting a pair of glasses, which she sometimes proudly wore around her neck, hanging on an old rusty-looking silver chain: Dolita knew she found them one day in the *basura*… (That's the rubbish bin by the way, for those of you who don't know any Spanish. As you will find quite a number of Spanish words in my story, I have put a simple Spanish/English glossary at the end of this book!)

Much to Dolita's amusement, she saw her rest them on the end of her nose from time to time: they were obviously a fashion accessory, a feel-good factor rather than purposeful, because Dolita knew that Old Ma Kensie could neither read nor write. As for what was happening in the street, she never missed a trick.

Ma Kensie was a survivor. She had to be. Having lived on the streets for many years there wasn't much she didn't know about that part of the city, and street life. Dolita would often sit with the old woman and listen to her stories. Sometimes she would sell flowers for her on the corner of *Plaza Mayor*. Dolita never knew how Ma Kensie came to acquire the flowers, but, as she shared the money from the sales, she didn't really care. That was her business and the few *pesos* from the flowers bought essentials for the "Street kids."

Whilst all the kids loved Ma Kensie, she played a very special part in Dolita's life. Why? Because Ma Kensie was the one who took care of Dolita from that first day when her mother left her on the city streets. Yes, the day when Taiawah left Dolita with the old woman. She left her at the doorway of the

Oficina de Ventas, supposedly for 10 minutes. But the truth is, she never came back. You would have to ask Taiawah why. I know Dolita will one day; that is, of course, assuming she ever sees her again.

Dolita hardly remembers her mum; she was so young, barely a year old. All Dolita knows and has known are the streets. So many questions. How did Old Ma Kensie take care of the young Dolita? Well, the fact is she did, and when Dolita was nearly five years old she went to live with the street kids at the shelter.

CHAPTER 4
THE STREET KID GANG

Before I continue with the story, allow me to introduce the characters and tell you a little about them.

OK, introducing the gang:

There are the twins, Manolo and Angelina, a little older than Dolita. Around nine-ish, there are no such

thing as birth certificates on the streets, so no one could be sure whether they were nine or ten years. Inseparable, it used to be hard to tell them apart and they have often been mistaken for one another. They wear the same attire, sweaters or baggy T-shirts, jeans and tennis shoes.

More recently Angelina seems to have been on a growth spurt and leaving Manolo behind. On the streets the girls usually look like the boys. Survival you know. Dolita, well she is different but Dolita is

Dolita after all. She is the only girl I know who wears a dress on the streets. Short cropped hair, baggy trousers, tatty jeans, baseball cap, are much more the norm. Being in the company of the twins for too long can become a strain on the most placid person because, although they clearly love one another, they squabble continuously. If you see one twin, there goes the other, two paces behind and Angelina is the one usually trailing behind. There she follows faithful in her brother's shadow. If she speaks to you at all you are honoured. She finds it difficult to make eye contact and number one brother usually speaks for both of them. The twins came to live on the streets because they had no father, well never knew him! And a mother with no income who was unable to take care of them. She became a prostitute to try to earn money and was found dead some time later. Murdered they say: never proved. Horrific! Consequently the kids ran away to the streets.

Then there is Roberto, 11-ish I think! Roberto

 never wears shoes, no never. Does not have a pair actually. Roberto is the one with the bonny face, not-so-clear complexion and the cheeky smile. He is very shy and spends most of the day sleeping, unless he is visiting the girl at the local hardware store. Roberto is really sweet on her, though she is far too old for him. He always wears the same navy coloured jogging bottoms with a hole in

the right buttock, a red baseball cap back-to-front and a huge sloppy sweater. Yes, even when it is very warm he still wears his oversized sloppy sweater. It is heaps too big for him and looks quite ridiculous actually. The sweater seems to be some sort of comfort as he somehow manages to wrap himself up in it at least twice. He sort of draws his arms up inside the sweater and hugs himself, hard to explain really. He has a habit of pulling it over his head to hide his face. A bit like a snail withdrawing into its shell I suppose you would say. When he is not sleeping and not at the store, he usually hangs around at the south entrance to the metro station. He is a predictable lad really. Never seems to cause any trouble, though he always has a cheeky grin and looks as though he is up to something even if he isn't. I don't think he would knowingly hurt anyone. Some people would say he is thick, others dozy: the truth is he snorts too much stuff and it is dulling his

senses, the brain cells slowly dying, I think! He's very slow to react and his speech is quite slurred. Mumbles a lot. His growth seems to have been stunted as well, 'cos he's really tiny compared to the other kids. Why is he on the streets? Don't ask!

Now Mikey; well he is a different story.

Dirty nails, black teeth and spiky hair. Rude, aggressive and bad-mannered, and that is on a

good day. Well OK, he cannot help the black teeth and dirty nails I suppose, but his attitude stinks. As I said, the street kids have a code, sort of a code of practice. Stick together; if you have something, share it; and all that stuff. Everyone seems to follow it, except Mikey that is. The other kids do not like him very much and his attitude has earned him the title of "Mikey Mean." It's a shame because he is one of the older boys and could be a great asset to the group if he were different. Unfortunately he is the troublemaker in the gang. Having known nothing but violence since he was a baby, he ran away from home to escape a violent stepfather and continuous beatings.

Now full of fear he always throws the first punch, often leaving the other guy startled. His opponent probably never intended to fight in the first place.

There is "Miggy Shoe Shine," so nicknamed because he is a shoe shiner. I suppose it didn't take much intelligence to work that one out. Everyone loves Miggy. A round chubby face, a smile from ear to ear and wild flyaway hair to match his wacky personality. Always happy, in spite of what life throws at him, he has a positive attitude. A talkative guy, always with something interesting to say.

Enrique is the oldest, about 17 years of age. He went away to live in a hostel for a few weeks, the Crisis Centre actually, and then returned to the shelter. At the hostel one of the workers taught him

a few words of English, which may or may not prove useful in the future; who knows? Yes, remember we are talking about the Street Kid gang here in Mexico City (one of many street kid gangs I might add) so their native language is Spanish. Not much call for English speaking on the streets. Enrique is the handsome one. *Guapo* or *mango*, we say in Mexico. He is the one who all the girls drool over, with his sleek black hair, attractive quiff, a melting smile and smouldering eyes, not to mention an excellent physique. With his dark brooding look, if cleaned up he could easily be mistaken for a Hollywood movie star. Most of all he dotes on Dolita, treats her like his precious little sister. Calls her his little buttercup and it drives her batty. Buttercup is *botón de oro* in Spanish, which translates "gold button," which is quite sweet don't you think? Enrique is what is known as a promoter, he works hand in hand with the guys at the Crisis Centre. Almost resigned himself to the fact that he is on the streets for life, as he tried to leave, but was unable to make the adjustments, he now watches out for the younger kids. He has rescued several *chiquitos* and young *chavos* from precarious and dangerous situations and taken them immediately to the safety of the Crisis Centre. He believes the streets are not the place for the kids and although he fears it's too late for him, he aims to do all he can to rescue others.

As for the rest of the kids. Hugh is about 15 years of age, has a stunning voice and loves to entertain. There's many a rags-to riches story been told in the world today. Imagine if he is the next one!

"Street Kid tops the charts!"

The others, well I am sure you will have the opportunity to meet some of them later. About 15 of them in total, all living in the shelter, mostly boys. Dolita, Angelina and Rocia are the only girls at the moment. Others

have stayed with them for a few weeks and then moved on. Dolita does not really bother with the others. Her real pals are the twins. Rocia is the motherly one; can't be described as a kid, but she lives with them. Overweight and plumpish, which is surprising because she never seems to eat anything. She looks typically

Indian, like a squaw, one of those lovely squaws that you see in the movies. She wears a colourful beaded braid around her head and she always has her long dark hair in plaits. She is the oldest and tries to keep the kids under control. No one knows how old she is, twenty something maybe. She just always seems to have been there. Rocia has a family that she goes to visit occasionally. She does not talk about her family much and no one dares to ask. She usually seems irritable and bad tempered when she has been away, so the other kids have learnt to mind their own business. If there is anything she wants them to know she will surely tell them. As I said, Rocia is the motherly one, the homemaker; I think you would call her.

Life would be dull without the animals.

Dogs, oh there are plenty of those on the streets. Their incessant barking drives you up the wall. When one starts they all follow. It is quite a dogs' chorus. The real characters are Raggy Man and Bozo, and the cat. Oh yes the cat with one eye. How could I forget the cat with one eye?

Raggy Man is sort of Dolita's dog, since he seems to have adopted her, and she him. They go almost

everywhere together. He is what you would call a little dog with a big, big character. His name is most befitting because he always looks such a 'raggy' mess.

Decidedly cute, he is renowned for his saucy expression and erect ears. Raggy Man is a wonderful companion, extrovert, mischievous and full of fun. A very intelligent little dog that loves adventure but is equally happy to lie by your side and enjoy your company and quiet moods. Quite yappy at times, Raggy Man is not in the least intimidated by large dogs.

The cat with one eye, well he does not have a name. He is just called "the cat with one eye," or "One-eye" for short. No one in the shelter knows where he lost his eye, or where Raggy Man came from for that  matter. They have just always been there.

Bozo, he is fairly new on the scene and is still settling in. A big dog, a cross between a German Shepherd and who knows what else! He could do with a real good wire brush 'cos his coat is oily and  he leaves tufts of long hair everywhere he goes. Bozo's coat (his fur that is; of course he doesn't wear a coat!) is so black that you can hardly see him in the dark. Smell him, well yes; that's another matter. He's desperately in need of a bath! Showing signs of a grumpy temperament, I suspect he will prove to be an excellent guard dog. "Guard dog?" I hear you say. "What is there to guard in a dirty old shelter?" - the kids themselves of course. If you were only eight or nine years old, living on the streets, you would probably be grateful for a dog like Bozo!

I suppose you might not like the shelter. Come to think of it, if you are reading this book, you will not like the shelter, especially if you live in one of those nice comfortable homes with all mod cons. You know the sort: cookers, washers, bath tubs, hot showers! Anyway the kids will make you welcome if you visit. To Dolita and the gang it's home.

If you are ever in Mexico City and want to find them, I'll give you a clue. Follow the dirt track down the side of the metro station and climb up the banking. No *necio*, won't tell you which metro station. If you want to find them badly enough you will. So let's be fair about this. The kids don't want too many visitors all at once. It would be a little overwhelming for them.

OK listen... Go round the back to what looks like some spare land and a dumping ground. Take a close look. There you will see a large plastic cover draped across the concrete pillars of the metro bridge. Look a little closer and you will see a gap in the plastic. Well, go in, don't be shy. They are only kids after all!

* * *

Urgh! Yes, I suppose if you live in one of those posh houses it is hard to stomach.

Smell? What smell? Just the smell of the streets and the...; and the ...!

Oh well, you would smell too if you never got bathed my dear. Too true, so don't criticise.

Now then, each kid has a carrier bag for his belongings. They hang from nails knocked into the shelter walls. What once was an elegant, very appealing tapestry, hangs crookedly on the rear wall. It depicted a simple Mexican village scene and the cloth, now faded and dirty, once boasted multitudes of highly-coloured birds, animals and insects. A couple of old beer barrels turned upside down provide tables and various sizes of crates and boxes substitute for chairs. Two or three double mattresses and a few blankets and pieces of foam salvaged from the local *basura* provide the basis of bedding for the fifteen kids. Needless to say several kids share a bed. The girls crash out on a different mattress. A bare bulb hangs from a wire which is straggled across the street. Connected to an old generator used by some of the market traders, it brings a touch of luxury to the shelter on market days. An old rusty oil stove supplies some heat on a cold damp night and Rocia uses it to cook some broth when she gets the ingredients.

That's about it, apart from a few personal possessions here and there, mainly belonging to Angelina who seems to be running her own "collectathon." Yes, under Angelina's part of the mattress there are all kinds of stuff and nonsense. Still, if it makes her happy and she is not hurting anyone, let her get on with it, that's what I say. Never a day goes by without she brings something back from the *basura*. The latest acquisition, a beaded pink handbag. I ask you, who wants a pink handbag?

Says she is saving it for when she gets off the streets and starts to dress like a girl. An interesting thought! She has sometimes found delightfully useful stuff; in fact, recently she returned with an old broken radio, which Dodgy Deunoro managed to repair.

Oh, he is the guy who has the lock-up round the corner. He calls it a garage. We call it a lock-up. Dodgy Deuno (for short)? Well I think I will tell you about him later…

So that basically is home. A couple of pictures, paintings of hope produced by Mexican school children, hanging crookedly on the concrete walls and the huge plastic sheet providing shelter from the elements. Yeah! That's home.

***

Now let's go back to the market as they continue to set up for the day and allow me to introduce you to the traders on *Calle Micalo*.

Romany Rosa and Papa Joe you have already met. There's Virginia, the scrawny girl who helps her mum with the fruit and veg, she looks needful of a good meal and Martinez who cannot seem to make his mind up whether he is a taxi driver or a market trader, probably because his old taxi seems to spend

 more time in Dodgy Deuno's lock-up than on the road.

It is one of those old green and white Volkswagen

Beetles. It must have been one of the first ever made I think! It seats two people in the back or three people at a squeeze and the passenger front seat has been removed to make the back seats more accessible. Martinez needs an alternative income, hence the stuff he sells on the market, usually bric-a-brac and bits of useful rubbish. Is there such a thing as useful rubbish? He has a sweet, petite wife, two young children and a new baby to feed.

The others, well don't much know them by name apart from Carlos who has the juice bar, and his brother who spends all day cooking and serving *burritos*. Miggy Shoe Shine sometimes helps out with the *burritos* when he's not shining shoes. Good combination, eh!

Hope he washes his hands in between jobs! As if!

As the morning advances *Calle Micalo* comes to life and the street rhythm takes shape. It's a lusty exuberant atmosphere. Busy, bustling, and the noise and chatter of the stallholders and their punters rises above the varying and differing tones of music. Some young hopefuls dressed *mariachi*-style wander down the street with an array of musical instruments including violin, guitar and trumpets. They hope to make enough to feed their families at least for the next couple of days. The youngest carries the begging bowl, the others playing to the best of their ability. Not the most awesome of performances but good enough to attract a crowd.

By noon the street is pulsing.

The smells and odours of the market rise in the morning air as cooking begins, the aroma of garlic and frying grasshoppers fighting for precedence over that of *enchiladas* stuffed with cheese and ham, *burritos* and various other local delights.

A man on the corner takes a swig of *tequila* and taps his foot to the rhythm of the *mariachi* music. The only thing more Mexican than *tequila* is *mariachi* and he is obviously intent on not having one without the other. Meant to be sipped like a fine cognac, another swig of the bottle, a quick gulp and it was gone. (He omitted to swallow the worm which is often found in a quality bottle of *tequila*!) Tossing the empty bottle aside he slowly slides down the lamp-post and slumps on the ground as though his world has just ended. A look of despair is painted on his face.

So this is the life and these are the people.

Virginia's mother catches a glimpse of Dolita and gives her a bag of soft fruit, remembering the time when the little Dolita, then only five years old, had stolen an apple and returned it. Her honesty had paid off and since that day Dolita has never been "fruit-less."

She climbs up the banking eating a succulent piece of mango and is greeted by the other kids who are just waking up, grateful to see her cheeky face and the bag of fruit that she is clutching in her grubby little hand.

So another day in the lives of the street kids begins.

CHAPTER 5
SURVIVAL

The story unfolds… Street life was never easy. Of course some days were better than others: each day held its own challenges and one thing was for sure, survival was the game. In parts the streets were a hive of activity, especially on market days with the hurry and bustle of the traders. Cooking smells guaranteed to fill the air as women, usually the Indian natives, set about cooking local dishes on the sidewalks. With their limited resources they were trying to make a living and it was surprising the numbers of passers-by and locals who would patronise them. That is providing you had some money of course! Something street kids rarely had and therefore to them, the next meal was never guaranteed. Frequently, the kids would go days without food. Hunger pains unfortunately took a hold, which led some of them in their desperation to steal. For others, picking pockets and snatching bags became the norm.

Dolita for the most part was good. She recalled that day however when she stole the apple from one of the market traders. The apples looked so inviting. She reached out and took the brightest and shiniest red apple she could see. (She was little more than five years old at the time.) She ran and dared not look back, but Dolita's conscience was later to get the better of her as she sheepishly returned it some time later. Do you know, hungry as she was, she didn't even take a bite? Holding out her hand she offered the apple to the old woman on the stall who looked at her with such amazement and bewilderment she told her to keep it anyway.

As I said earlier, from that day on the old woman often gave Dolita a piece of fruit and their friendship blossomed. The woman turned out to be young Virginia's mum. News soon spread amongst the traders and Dolita's honesty, plus the fact that she was cute and adorable in a mischievous sort of way, soon earned her the respect of all the traders in the *Calle Micalo*. Some days the kids were fortunate enough to be given other food stuffs, a handful of nuts or beans, a piece of raw veg, even a stick of liquorice was gratefully accepted. Handouts tended to be twice weekly, Tuesday and Friday; market days. All thanks to Dolita! Only the Street Traders in *Calle Micalo* gave food to the kids; other market traders ignored them. They were trying to make a meagre living themselves. Oh yes, life on the streets was all about survival and that was something every street kid and street trader learnt.

Miggy Shoe Shine was no exception. He had a survival strategy and he was determined to see it through. At the age of 11 years Miggy had a business plan. He started collecting bottles, glass, plastic; basically anything that could be re-used or recycled. Each week, Miggy spent hours at the city dump, day after day searching for stuff. Then, after sorting and sifting, it would be collected later by a dealer who gave him a few *pesos* for his time. Miggy in his wisdom decided not to tell anyone about his plan until it was more advanced and he hid the *pesos* in a hole in the mattress at the shelter.

Each time Miggy had collected enough he went out and bought something for his business. First the brushes, and then the cloths, later, of course, some shoe shine cream. You may be thinking they won't cost much, but remember any money he managed to come by would normally be spent on food; without a doubt! He was very annoyed when someone found his secret stash and took the shoeshine cream. He suspected that it must be one of the new kids that had recently joined them because he knew none of the others would do such a mean thing. As a consequence he found a new hiding place and started saving again. Finally, having had a decidedly fortunate day, he found himself a small wooden box with a lid and a handle. Carefully placing all the items in the box, Miggy was ready and set off to find his first customer . . .

It was 8.30am, a good time to catch the office workers he thought, and he waited on the corner of the *Plaza Mayor*. The first person to come along was a tall chap, well dressed, with briefcase and paper in hand. Miggy jumped out in front of him shouting, "Shoe shine sir?"

"My goodness, you *necio*, you startled me!" said the man and pushed Miggy out of the way.

"*******," thought Miggy! "Let's try again. Shoe shine sir?"

One hour later and no shoes to shine, Miggy was beginning to think this was not such a good idea after all. One hour passed. Two hours passed; no shoes to shine. Miggy began to feel downcast and then - suddenly his breakthrough came!

"Hey you boy," came a voice from across the street.

"Can you shine my shoes?"

"Yes sir, sure will sir," cried Miggy and sped across the street, dodging a yellow bicycle hurtling round the corner. Flinging open his box, reaching for a cloth, he eagerly began to clean the man's shoes.

This was to be the beginning of his enterprising little business, which ultimately led to his name of course - "Miggy Shoe Shine." His face became known by most businessmen who passed through the *Plaza Mayor* and each in turn stopped for a shoeshine. Even some of the women patronised him, though it was rare to see a woman on the streets having her shoes cleaned.

I'll give you an insight into the future.

Miggy's story has a happy ending and his shoe shining business grows into his car cleaning enterprise. Yes, the same man who had commissioned his first ever shoe shine, one year later says to Miggy,

"Hey you boy, can you make that car shine as good as these shoes?"

Whilst Miggy is still living in the shelter he is determined that by 16 he will have a proper roof over his head and will not live the life of a street kid!

Go for it Miggy that's what I say!

Dolita, by far the youngest of the kids, often showed herself to be the most sensible. She knew so much stuff, having wisdom far beyond her years. When you asked how she knew things she always shrugged her shoulders, giggled and answered, "Just do."

"It's as though she has been here before," said Old Ma Kensie, though only joking. Ma Kensie certainly did not believe in reincarnation.

"We get one chance here," she would say, "then absent from the body, present with the LORD. That's for those who believe of course!"

Whatever that meant and who the lord was, Dolita had no idea. One day she would take time to find out.

It was because Dolita was so sensible that the other kids were amazed when she took off and did something a little crazy, and this particular day was one of those days. It was eight in the morning and Miggy collected his belongings ready to go to the *Plaza Mayor* once again. Dolita decided to walk with him, calling, Raggy Man, to accompany her. Having sat around for a while at the *plaza* and watching the world go by she said goodbye to Miggy and moved on just as his first punter arrived. Raggy Man followed faithfully by her side. The street kids always greeted each other and said goodbye with their own individual handshake.

A slap with the palm of the right hand, the palm of each kid forced together. Then with an upward stroking movement, retrieving their hand and clenched fist coming back again to knock their knuckles together. Another slap with the palm of the right hand.

If you didn't get that then read it again!

"*Hasta*," said Dolita, smiling mischievously and off she went.

Dolita rarely went anywhere without Raggy Man, particularly when she went to the dump because he had an expert eye, or should I say a nose, for all things good. Feeling extremely hungry she decided to cut through the market at *Calle Calypso*, praying that one of the traders would pass something her way; unlikely, but nevertheless she was hopeful.

Walking down The Strip, so called because it was such a narrow lane, with bars and tobacconists either side, she jumped for joy when one of the juice boys gave her a drink. The fact that it was thick tomato juice and she hated the taste of the stuff was irrelevant. Beggars can't be choosers and Dolita was grateful for anything. Juice bars were common in the city. Selling all types of juices made from freshly squeezed fruit and vegetables, the bars were often patronised by the walkers passing by to their offices. Raggy Man looked at her expectantly; he usually took the opportunity to share anything going. A lick of the lips, he soon lost his nose in the remnants of the plastic glass. With a shudder he backed off as though something in the glass had spat back at him. Dolita howled with laughter at the comical expression: the look of disgust. The sticky red juice was all around his chops and up his nose. "How I love that little dog," she thought, wiping his face with the corner of her already dirty, stained dress. Then, clicking her fingers, she let him know they were going on their way again.

Nearing Calypso, Dolita began to notice a strong police presence and, as she turned the corner, to her dismay found there was no market. Umm! No market meant - no lunch! She would have to come up with another idea. This was most unfortunate as by now she had been up for more than three hours and was ravenously hungry. street kids certainly never had regular meals. They ate when the opportunity arose, which was all or nothing. The police presence indicated that something was going down or was about to happen and she didn't want to stay around long enough to find out what.

"OK, plan B," she thought, turning around and heading for *Casa Gonzalez*, near Beeky's house.

It was several weeks since Dolita had seen Beeky and her pace quickened at the thought of seeing the loveable old woman and possibly getting to taste some of her home made *burritos* and *guacamole*. Well, she could dream! Beeky was not wealthy but, having more than sufficient, she would certainly help the street kids if at all possible, especially those who tried to help themselves, Dolita of course being one of them. Beeky's little house was pretty. Painted white, with large indigo-blue gates and bronze-coloured iron railings, it was adjacent to *Casa Gonzalez*, the grand guesthouse used by tourists and businessmen on the *Calle San Felipe*. Here, Dolita did something totally out of character, and quite foolish!

CHAPTER 6
BEEKY'S HOUSE

The house was dark inside. Small quaint rooms with low ceilings, corners and alcoves, lots of ornately carved pieces of furniture: wooden, sturdy but lacking in colour. Beeky usually kept the shutters down to screen out the sun. Not that there was much sun in this part of town: it struggled to break through the smog.

Beeky was a sweet-looking character, who always had her legs bandaged from the ankle to the knee. Dolita never did ask why. Some things are just better kept personal. San Felipe was a pleasant *calle* with several pretty houses all well cared for; quite a contrast to those on neighbouring streets. Amazingly, Mexico City was full of surprises. A city described as "one of many contrasts," you often didn't get what you expected.

Because of the absolute extremes of wealth and poverty, most of those who were well-off didn't like to advertise the fact. Modesty was considered a virtue and the wealthy consequently lived behind tall walls that concealed all from their neighbours. It was not that the neighbours didn't know, but it wasn't considered prudent and most certainly unkind to rub ones noses in it. Much is hidden in the city, where many things turn out to be quite different from how they might first appear.

Beeky's house was one of those with hidden virtues, though modest in comparison to many. To the front of the house was a very tiny garden. The tall gates were always locked and a large sign on the main gatepost warned, "Beware of the dog." Funny really, because Dolita knew Beeky's dog and he was as soft as a brush; certainly more likely to lick you with admiration than defend Beeky's property against intruders. The only way to the rear of the house was through the main entrance, down the passageway and out at the other side. (Through the house itself, I mean.) There was no walkway around it. Good for security no doubt, but a flipping nuisance when there was lots of garden rubbish to get rid of. Fortunately Beeky's garden didn't boast much rubbish. It was very well maintained and she had the prettiest little garden surrounding a small square courtyard. The prettiest little garden you ever did see. A blue and white pebbled mosaic path meandered from the door to the far end of the garden. Beeky obviously liked blue because a small natural style pond in the far corner was enhanced with an outer ring of blue pebbles of varying shapes and sizes. A semi-wild area, it was perfect for birds that could be seen darting in and out of the water. (When Beeky's cat was nowhere to be seen of course!)

Dolita felt it impossible not to unwind and chill when she sat in the precious little garden, listening to the trickle and soft sounds of the tiny waterfall in the pond. There was always something very relaxing about the sound of running water she thought. An appropriate description of the waterfall was that of a wall fountain. Three cisterns of pouting faces spouted water that cascaded down into the pond to be recirculated by a pump. A remarkable idea and, by the style and age of the cisterns, something which had been in the garden for many years. The pond, in fact, had most of the water surface covered by water lilies, water hyacinths and other flowers which floated, forming a carpet of stunning colours.

A tiny decked courtyard made a stunning centrepiece, with a gazebo to the far left. Dolita loved to sit in the gazebo, which was now quite overgrown with trailing ivy and a Russian vine. A circular bench around the whole perimeter of the gazebo made it a lovely little hideaway. An empty circular bird cage hung in the corner, which once housed two small love birds - before Beeky's cat came along and frightened them to death that is.

The rest of the garden consisted of fragrant sprays of white tobacco plants, and a large clump of fiery-red monardas. With trifid-like petals, they looked as though they were from another planet. There was an abundance of yellow roses, all just bursting into bloom, and an overgrown lemon tree bowed with the weight of the lemons, many of which had fallen to the ground and were now being eaten by ants and other grateful insects. This secluded and tranquil spot, tucked away in the city garden, made it so easy to lose oneself; particularly for a street kid, to forget the drudgery and sadness of the streets and the burdens of the outside world. The whole garden was an absolute delight with perfumes from the various flowers all fighting to be the dominant aroma.

Dolita's thoughts of seeing Beeky and sitting in the garden quickened her pace. Raggy Man's little legs speeded up and his tail wagged eagerly. He was always happy to go out with Dolita and recognised the way to Beeky's house. Immediately turning into *Calle San Felipe* the sound of raised voices could be heard. A man unknown to Dolita was sitting on the roof of Beeky's house. Thankfully the rooftops in *Calle San Felipe* were quite low. It was evident from the conversation and the various tins of paint scattered around that he had been painting the house.

Seemingly a quarrel had developed about the cost of the job and Beeky had apparently refused to pay. In anger he had climbed to the top of the chimney-pot and was painting it black. Her lovely pristine, freshly painted white house, and he was now painting the chimney-pot black! It looked horrible. It looked quite ridiculous, but Dolita had to giggle. Beeky glared at her. Oops; no chance of the *burritos* now, she thought, and apologised to Beeky, who was pleased to see her but clearly quite distressed.

Well, Beeky did invite Dolita in. The painter remains unpaid and the chimney-pot is black to this day, causing a point of discussion for all those who pass by. Dolita spent the remainder of a very pleasant day with Beeky.

* * *

"You want something to eat?" asked Beeky.

"Oh please," answered Dolita, "*¡Tengo mucha hambre!*"

Beeky laughed. "I thought as much."

She did not have the *burritos* and *guacamole*, but Beeky opened a large tin of sardines, smothered in rich tomato sauce, which they shared with the cat. Yes, Raggy Man had one too, even though it was that dreaded tomato stuff again.

"One-eye would like these," said Dolita, as Beeky raised her eyebrows and looked towards her.

"Don't see One-eye around 'ere much these days," she replied, cutting a chunky slice off a small crusty brown loaf and passing it to Dolita to eat with the sardines. A dollop of homemade *mermelada de frambuesa* was at the side of the plate waiting to be spread on the bread. Dolita stuck her finger into the *mermelada*. It tasted delicious.

"Used to be often around 'ere; don't suppose he goes so far now he is getting older."

"How old is One-eye?" questioned Dolita.

"Don't really know. He always seems to have been around until for some reason he started inhabiting the shelter where you street kids live."

"I wonder what happened to his eye?"

"Don't you know?" exclaimed Beeky. "Well, I will tell you. It was one particular night in January and it was bitterly cold. One-eye, who then of course had two eyes, climbed into the engine of an old station wagon to keep warm."

"How did he do that?"

"He climbed in from underneath."

"Oh!"

"Well, the story goes, a young man, not known to me I might add, the owner of the station wagon, decided to go out unexpectedly during the night. It is said that he turned on the engine to hear a yelp and a squeal."

"Ooh, sounds awful!"

"It was! For the cat anyway. He was lucky to be alive. Needless to say, he lost the sight in his right eye."

Dolita shuddered, thinking she had just lost her appetite, but nevertheless forced herself to eat the crusty bread and sardines. It might be a long time before she ate again.

Dolita decided not to rush back to the shelter and stayed with Beeky until nearly nightfall, in spite of the fact that she usually liked to be at the shelter before dark. It was really quite dangerous for her to be out on her own, even with Raggy Man. Beeky busied herself in and out of the garden and Dolita pottered, helping her with various domestic chores. She felt content and blissfully happy. Beeky's cat having disappeared for a while, left the garden filled with the chatter and sounds of the birds. Something looking rather like a hedgehog strolled across the grass and Raggy went potty. Fortunately for the hedgehog, on this occasion Raggy was more yap than action and decided he didn't want to play with it. Beeky's dog slept most of the afternoon and took no interest in either Dolita or Raggy Man, surprisingly enough.

Beeky had an old wicker basket in which she kept her small collection of needles and thread. Dolita loved to rummage through the basket, admiring the different cottons and silks and asked Beeky shyly if she would sew up the latest hole in her old brown dress. Beeky found a perfect piece of orange material, which would make a fine patch, and it was just the right size to cover the hole. As it was a warm afternoon Beeky gave Dolita one of her old cotton blouses to wear temporarily. She laughed. Dolita did look rather ridiculous, but needs must and she took the dress, washed, repaired it and placed it on the line to dry. Sitting back in her rickety cane garden chair, Beeky then took a well-earned nap.She was nearly 80 years old after all and had worked very hard all that day. Dolita chuckled, as her old friend was soon fast asleep, sounding more like an old bear than an old woman. With every breath she snored, inhaling and exhaling, causing the chair to shift position and creak. Dolita looked around for something to occupy her time until her dress was dry and Beeky had taken her nap. She had a brilliant idea.

Or was it?

She decided she would pierce her ears, but how? With a needle of course, out of Beeky's sewing box. She had often thought how she would love to wear earrings like some of the posh ladies and this was her chance. Surely Beeky would not mind. Oooh, but what if it hurts, she thought? An idea came into her head and slowly and quietly she slipped through the garden door, entered Beeky's kitchen and passed through to the scullery, which housed the fridge. The one room in the house that was really bright and colourful was the kitchen. In the centre was a large wooden pine table. It was an old farmhouse style and was very heavy. With it stood four very sturdy looking chairs and an old wooden stool. The kitchen was fitted with cupboards and drawers of various shapes and sizes and, guess what? They were all painted blue. Sky blue! A large dresser full of memorabilia was also painted the same blue. Obviously Beeky liked blue but the rest of the house was quite dull in comparison to the kitchen. The focal point of the kitchen was an ancient, double sized Aga and a huge pan of beans stood, soaking on one of the gas rings. A water purifier on the wall nearby looked in need of repair.

The smell of sardines lingered in the kitchen and several jars of varying types of freshly made *mermelada* were cooling on the table. Resisting the urge to stick her fingers in each one and take a scoop as she passed by, she turned her attention to the tiny, cluttered scullery and a large cube of ice from the fridge. Hoping that Beeky would not be angry with her for wandering around the house, Dolita held it to her left ear for quite some time. The ear naturally went numb. Dolita pinched it and felt nothing. Good! Needle in hand she pushed it through the lobe being careful to look at her reflection in a small mirror on the scullery wall. "Well that was easy!" she thought and repeated the procedure with the other ear, dabbing the trickle of blood with a piece of paper towel. A little yucky, but she didn't feel a thing.

"Oh dear!" Dolita gasped, "How stupid. Now what do I do? I have nothing to put in the holes. No earrings. Now what?"

Looking in the sewing box, to her absolute delight she found two of the prettiest little gold safety pins ever.

"Well, these will make very fine earrings until I get some real ones." And quick as a flash she put the delicate, tiny pins through her ears and sat back to marvel at her achievement. The whole thing had been very easy and, apart from the fact that her ears felt cold, she had felt nothing. Simple!

An hour passed; Dolita's dress dried whilst she played with Raggy Man in the garden. Beeky began to stir and the numb cold feeling in Dolita's ears was beginning to wear off and they were starting to smart. Only slightly, but nevertheless they were beginning to pain her. She flicked her hair over her ears, quickly concealing the evidence of her exploit and hid the bloody paper towels in Beeky's waste bin. After spending a little more time with Beeky she gratefully thanked her for the bread and sardines, also for washing and sewing the dress. Giving Beeky a big hug she left, with Raggy Man once again by her side. Trundling home through the dark, by the time they reached the shelter Dolita was in a considerable amount of pain.

"Anything the matter?" questioned Rocia, who expected to see the delight on Dolita's face when she showed her the huge ham bone that one of the market traders had given her.

"Lots of meat on 'ere," she said, "and we have bread too. Tonight, girl, we feast!"

Dolita smiled weakly trying to show her enthusiasm.

"Wow," she said, and muttered something about sardines.

"What are you talking about girl, what's that about sardines? What is wrong with you anyway?" Rocia asked, looking at Dolita curiously. "This isn't like you. Has someone upset you or something?" she asked, suddenly feeling all protective."

"No," whispered Dolita, in a husky voice, "I did it myself."

"Did what?"

Dolita flicked back her hair to reveal her latest fashion accessory. Looking more closely at the tiny gold safety pins in Dolita's ears, Rocia thought at first that the mischievous little girl was playing a prank. She soon realised it was for real. The evidence of dried blood and swelling to one ear clearly revealed what she had done.

"Oh, heavens above! What you done girl? Why do you want your ears piercing anyway?" she asked.

"Just do," came the feeble reply

It goes without saying the next few days proved to be quite an ordeal with two infected ears, a considerable amount of pain and Rocia playing out her role as the motherly one, yet again. Taking the sap from an aloe vera plant growing nearby, Rocia treated Dolita's ears: gently rubbing the thick sticky gel into each ear lobe, applying it every few hours, the infection finally subsided. The two safety pins went in the trashcan. This was not the first time that the sticky white substance taken from the inside of the aloe vera plant had come to the rescue of one of the street kids.

"Its good stuff," said Rocia, who knew lots about natural remedies.

CHAPTER 7
THE HOUSE AT 247

As the days and weeks passed, life was a mixture of emotions. Sadness, misery, pain, but also joy and excitement. Dolita took pleasure in the simple things and the camaraderie in a game of cards or marbles. "Crystalline baubles that flatter the eye." The game that does not need sophistication, with as few as two players, or as many as you like. The different types of marbles, some brightly coloured, others opaque. The favourites were those with the three leaves simulated in the centre; a game not as popular as it used to be but one loved by the kids at the shelter. The marbles court was a place of dirt, just a small stick to trace the line, the mark from which the crystal balls should be tossed: a small hole as the goal. The kids played on.

Manolo came charging into the shelter with a story of an abandoned house that he had discovered and wanted them to visit.

"Where is this house?" Dolita asked with great enthusiasm.

"247 *Los Olivos*, the corner of *Calle Don Jose*. Come on, get a move on, it will be dark soon. *¡Rápido! ¡Rápido!*" said Manolo, tugging on the arm of his twin sister.

"*¿Qué onda? ¿Qué onda?*" grunted Roberto annoyed that Manolo was causing such a commotion and disturbing his sleep.

58

"¡*Vamos a ver!*" said Dolita eagerly.

"Well count me out," mumbled Roberto," I wanna sleep."

"Oh don't be such a bore! All you ever do is sleep!" exclaimed Dolita.

"Not much else to do around 'ere," he replied.

"You could play marbles," giggled Angelina. He looked mortified.

"Big deal!"

"Well now, seems there is something to do for once! Come on Roberto, try and look interested! And do take your arms out of that horrendous sweater and put it on properly," said Dolita.

"¡*Vale!* OK! OK!" mumbled Roberto, shrugging his shoulders. "It better be good!" and off they went. The twins taking the lead, Dolita and Roberto and one of the other kids followed behind.

"Perhaps we should have waited for the others," said Dolita. "We might need one of the older ones. What if we get into a fix?" she exclaimed, realising that in her eagerness for adventure, she had not given too much thought to the situation.

"Oh shut up, Dolita," said Manolo. "We're only going to take a closer look, then we'll come back with the others later."

It seemed to take forever to get to the corner of *Calle Don Jose*. The twins knew all the short cuts but Dolita still didn't like the idea of being so far away from the shelter, particularly as it was now quite late in the afternoon. She had never felt comfortable in this part of town. Their walking pace speeded up until Dolita felt quite exhausted. She really wished she had stayed behind, but would have hated to miss something that could prove to be exciting. After all she had been the enthusiastic one initially. Little Raggy Man was puffing and panting but keeping close to her heels.

"Nearly there," said Manolo. "Just round this corner and across the *plaza.*"

A huge sigh of relief from Dolita, a yap of approval from Raggy Man as though he understood every word and delight on Angelina's face.

"Thank goodness," mumbled Roberto, "Could've been sleeping! Mmm! Better be good! What's wrong with the shelter anyway? Who wants to move? Not me!"

"Oh do be quiet. We are not moving, and can't you talk properly instead of that constant mumbling?" said Manolo, glaring at Roberto. Quite suddenly, as the *calle* came to an abrupt and unexpected end, he pointed to the old door and the rusty nameplate hidden by foliage on the gatepost at the side. "*¡Mira!*"

It didn't look like a house at all from where they were standing. They could easily have missed the house it was so well hidden; in fact it did not look much like a house at all, with no windows to be seen and a large rusty iron grille across the door. The kids peered wondering how they were going to get in.

"*Casa Ana Maria 247.*"

"So who lives here?" asked Roberto

"No one of course, *necio.* It's abandoned. Remember, Manolo told you."

"It's been empty for over a year!"

"How do you know?" asked Dolita.

"Just do," Manolo said, winking at Dolita, knowing that was her favourite catchphrase.

"So how do we get in?" she asked.

"This way, follow me and make sure no one sees you."

He soon disappeared round the back of the building which was so well hidden, with large conifers, easily seven metres tall, knitting together to form an excellent security hedge and screen. At the far side of the house, prising his way between the conifers through the tiniest of gaps, into the vast array of bushes and undergrowth, he entered the garden at the rear. The others followed. The garden was so wildly over-grown with tall straggly weeds and un-kempt grass. The windows were shadowed by an exceptionally large lemon tree, which proceeded to tower above the roof of the house. A selection of large earthenware pots were scattered around the doorway and all the windows had steel security grilles.

Dolita looked at one of the pots that had a name and some dates inscribed on the rim.

She shuddered.

"Oh yuk!" she exclaimed casting it aside quickly, wondering what type of gruesome contents it might hold and certainly not caring to find out.

"This door is so old and rotten," said Manolo, pointing to a door whose security grille had once been prised away from the wall with something similar to an iron bar, possibly by would-be burglars.

"I've kicked it in, did it when I came down earlier. You sure no one saw you enter the garden?"

"Yeah," replied the others simultaneously.

"OK. This is ours, finders keepers and all that stuff," and in they all squeezed through a half metre square hole in the bottom of the door.

"Urgh gross! It smells awful, like there's a dead cat or something in here," said Dolita as she found herself to be the second one to enter the house.

"Probably is! Only joking…" laughed Manolo, looking at Dolita's horrified expression in the dim light.

"It'll be getting dark soon," mumbled Roberto, yawning nervously.

"Ought to be getting back. Don't really wanna cross this part of town in the dark. You know the Molina brothers and their gang hang about around 'ere and they are trouble man. Come to think of it, I'm surprised they haven't found this place before us."

"Well they have not!" snapped Manolo. Dolita looked uncomfortable. The Molinas' reputation preceded them.

"Relax, they're all packed up; moved about a week ago. Gone to the outer city, camping somewhere near the city dump. In an old caravan I'm told."

Dolita sighed, "What a relief!"

"Never seen the Molina brothers," said the kid who had accompanied them. His name was Javier and he was quite new to the shelter.

"You don't want to see them," replied Manolo, "but you'll sure know if you do."

"How?"

"The way they dress for starters. Red waistcoats, black leather jackets and sleeked back hair. Oh and yes, they have steel cap toes on their boots. You don't want a kick from one of them!"

"I'm sure glad they're out of town," said Javier shuddering. Dolita nodded in agreement. Angelina was oblivious to the conversation and was by now exploring the house.

A sigh of relief from Roberto, a quick look round and they all agreed to go, in spite of the fact that their adventure had barely begun. They couldn't see much; it was now too dark. Old burgundy velveteen curtains and pieces of dirty material were strung across the windows. That along with the huge overgrowth and antique wooden shutters restricted most of the light. They all agreed that they would return the next day with the older kids.

"Strange," said Dolita, as they were walking back, her feet throbbing. "It looks as though whoever lived there left in a real hurry. They left everything behind. Did you notice the house was full of stuff?"

"Drr… of course," said Manolo. "That's why I took you there."

"OK clever clogs, but you might have told us it was such a long way!" complained Dolita, taking off her ill-fitting shoes and carrying them.

"Yeah, I looked in the dresser. There were sheets, blankets, towels and some kid's books in another cupboard that I opened."

They all looked in amazement. Angelina rarely spoke, usually hanging onto her brother's arm and allowing him to be the mouthpiece for both of them. Now she was very excited, quite a pain really, they could hardly shut her up.

"There were books in the other room as well," she said.

"Uhm! Not much good to us," mumbled Roberto. "Can anyone 'ere read?"

"Well, we can still enjoy the pictures!" snapped Angelina, her upper lip curling, and looking hurt.

He was not impressed. "Books! Who wants books? Would rather sleep! Suppose we could use them to stoke a fire!"

Angelina tutted in exasperation; Dolita giggled.

Some time later, back at the shelter Dolita's mind wandered. She thought about the house and when they would go back. She thought she would like some books. Actually she thought she would like to learn to read. Yes, she would like to learn to read, but who would teach her? She lay down, closed her eyes, lost in her dreams she fell asleep.

The next morning everyone was awake earlier than usual. Strange! Even Roberto was ready to go.

"That's a turnaround for you," said Manolo. "What's up? Can't sleep?" Roberto made no comment.

This time some of the older *chavos* came too and they set off once again for the house at 247. Nine of them in all, they split up into 3 groups so as not to be too conspicuous. Large numbers of kids crossing town attracted too much attention. This time they seemed to reach the *Calle Don Jose* more quickly, round the corner and across the *plaza*, the house at 247 loomed in the distance.

Dolita and the twins took the lead. A soft whistle signalled the others to follow. They scrambled through the gap in the conifers, which Manolo had carefully concealed the night before. Crawling on their knees into the huge overgrown garden, then, sliding on their bellies through the broken door, they went into the house once again. "Yuk, it smells!" said Hugh pinching his nose.

"Umh, we know that," giggled Dolita. "Dead cats!" She giggled again, seeing the expression on some of their faces.

"It's so dark," said one of the older boys, nearly falling over Dolita and pushing her out of the way.

"Open the shutters," mumbled Roberto.

"Oh, that's very sensible Roberto!" said Manolo sarcastically. "Don't be so stupid everyone will see us."

Roberto shrugged his shoulders and sat down on the first thing resembling a chair that he could find. It collapsed and he fell in a heap on the floor. The others howled with laughter.

"Who's going to see us in here?" he puzzled. "This place is so well hidden no one can see the house let alone who's in it! Drr......."

"OK, where's the kitchen?" asked Hugh, glad that he had thought to borrow a torch from Deuno earlier, knowing that he had only let him borrow it 'cos he said it was for Dolita!

"This way, I found it," whispered another kid and they all piled into the kitchen. Hugh began to open cupboards one by one, shining the torch and displaying their contents. There was a damp musty smell, *cucarachas*, ants and other critters scuttled away as the brightness of the light disturbed their habitat.

"What you all watching me for?" he asked, realizing that everyone was peering over his shoulder. "This is like a comedy act. Scatter and see what you can find and remember, we are street kids, *chavos* to the core. No such thing as finders' keepers. We share everything!" Hugh was now seemingly taking charge of the whole operation.

"Even with them Molina brothers?" questioned Manolo.

"Don't be such a *necio*. Our gang of course; what we find we share so don't be so stupid. Disappear and see what you can find!"

Dolita didn't know how long they had been in the house, but it felt too long. She was feeling nervous and wanted to leave. She didn't like to take anything out of the house, just wanted a nosey around. It was an adventure to her, but stealing? No. She would take some books, borrow them and bring them back. Yes, what a good idea. She would bring them back when she had learnt to read.

"What's wrong?" questioned Manolo.

"Yeah, what's wrong?" echoed his sister. They had both noticed that Dolita was the only one not stashing things in a bag to take away.

"It's stealing."

"What…?! Get real Dolita. You take things every day that are not yours!"

"Yes, but from the *basura*; things people don't want."

"So, they don't want these if they have been gone a year."

"What's the difference?" exclaimed Manolo, stuffing all kinds of everything into his bag.

"It's only a matter of time before someone else finds this place and if it's the Molina brothers they will soon empty it."

"But…" "No buts Dolita. If you have a conscience so be it. I sometimes really do wonder how you survive on the streets."

"Well I do. Just do!" she shrugged.

"Uhm… well if you change your mind I found these."

Manolo handed her a pair of shoes. They looked just her size and were clearly new. Good solid shoes, black, shiny and perfect. Dolita had never had any shiny shoes; in fact she had never had any new shoes. She looked down at the pair that she wore which were very tatty. They were given to her when she discarded her last pair and now these too let in the rain and rubbed her feet. Well, maybe, just maybe she could take the shoes. By the time the owner came back they probably would not fit anyway and she did need some shoes. Actually they were just perfect for her, so shoes in one hand, books in another, Dolita and the kids were nearly ready to leave.

"Put them on," said Manolo

"Later," grinned Dolita, looking at the shoes proudly.

"Well where's the logic in that?" he muttered.

"OK then," said Dolita.

The house undoubtedly had been like Aladdin's cave. The kids had so much stuff they could not possibly carry another thing. Roberto's baggy sweater came in most useful as he stuffed it full and tied a knot in it around his waist.

"You're *loco* man!" said Manolo, though he had to agree that it was a rather ingenious idea. Manolo had various tins of food: apricots, peaches and anchovies. Some warm blankets and various items of clothing. He had no idea that the use-by date on the tins was two years out of date. He couldn't read, nor would he have cared he was always so hungry.

The older boys had some pots and pans, something that resembled a kettle but wasn't a kettle, a new tin opener, because the shelter opener was rusty, and some strange-looking bottles of "plonk." Roberto found himself another sweater and, to his delight, a pack of playing cards alongside some strange looking board games.

And there was more and there was more and there was more! A house full of treasures! Trash or treasure, to them it was all treasure!

"I wonder what's in 'ere?" questioned Hugh as he reached to pull on the handle of what seemed to be a trap door smack in the centre of the passageway. It must have been hidden under the old rustic rug that one of the kids had disturbed.

"Oooh, scary," said one of the gang.

"Help me open it, help me open it," urged Hugh, tugging with all his might on the handle.

It took one sharp tug by three of them and it was open. Hugh shone his torch in the space that appeared to be no more than a dirty hole.

Angelina had another useless handbag, which thrilled her and some more pictures and plastic flowers to decorate the shelter walls. Her prize possession was a beautiful "looking glass," a mirror so to speak. About 30 cm long and so beautiful she held the indigo-blue handle and allowed her fingers to trace the pattern of the ornately painted flowers on the rear. Holding it up to her face and turning it around she looked curiously at her reflection. Was she pretty or did she look like a boy? Suddenly interrupted by the shouts of the others, she knew they had found something of interest and put down the looking glass. She sped over to join them.

Meanwhile, Dolita had wandered into another room, a strange little room adjacent to the kitchen. It had clearly been used as a bedroom and housed two rickety single beds with dirty blue cotton throw-overs. An ancient-looking pine chest of drawers was wedged between them and she opened the top drawer to see what delights she might find inside. Nothing! Blast, there was nothing! She meandered off.

"It's full of rubbish!" exclaimed Hugh.

Disappointment on their faces, by now Dolita had joined the others. Pushing her way through and looking into the space below the trap door, she yelled,

"That's not rubbish!"

"How do you know that?"

"Just do."

"Well it sure looks like rubbish to me."

"Well, if someone took the trouble to hide it here it must be of value!"

She pulled out the mass of papers and, there underneath, discovered a slim oblong box about 30 cm in length, 15 cm in width and 7 or 8 cm deep. It appeared to be locked and the small gold lock was rusty and corroded. Indeed the box was very old and dirty. She began to search around for the key but to no avail.

"Take the lot," said Hugh, snatching it from her and stuffing it all into his huge plastic bag.

"Mmm..! Interesting! We'll look through it later," he said while closing the trap door and concealing the hiding place once again with the old rug.

CHAPTER 8
DEVNORO'S LOCK-UP

Back at the shelter the box was forgotten until the following day. Sorting through what could only be described as the spoils of the previous day's escapades, Hugh once again came across the box. Dolita lay curled up with Raggy Man, thinking about the house and how strangely peaceful it had felt; yet there had been an eeriness too. She longed to know its secrets: who had lived there? Why had they gone away and left everything behind? So strange that they had not packed up their belongings! Had they left in a hurry? All these questions circling in her head.

Hugh placed the box on the floor and was just about to stamp on it to break it open as Dolita leapt forward and pushed him aside.

"No," she shouted. "Don't damage it."

She recalled having noticed a carving or an inscription the day before, She remembered the letter T at least, and some other illegible writing on the base. Rescuing the box from Hugh's fiery grip and taking an old rag, dipping it into the rusty water barrel outside the shelter, she began to clean it. Rubbing carefully, concentration and anticipation written all over her face, the wooden box began to lose its dirty old appearance and shine in parts where it was less worn.

It must have once been bright and decorative, but now, any original colour was very much faded. True enough, it was delicately carved with the shape of an eagle on the lid, and the initials T.C.S. clearly inscribed on the base. Other small birds and animals were carved on the sides. What once looked as though they had been cheerful pink, white, tangerine and rich burgundy flowers were hand-painted in other parts. Even if the box were empty Dolita knew that it must be hundreds of years old and that it would be a shame to destroy it. Someone had laboured for several hours to decorate its appearance, and it was quite exquisite.

Looking up at Hugh's curious expression she suggested that she take the box to Dodgy Deuno's. He was sure to have a key. Deuno had a collection of keys to fit all shapes and sizes. Failing that, at least he would be able to open the box with a piece of wire or something. She was determined not to damage the box and Dolita had every faith in Dodgy Deuno's ability to open it.

Hugh thought it was a load of fuss about nothing but as it seemed so important to Dolita, he agreed to humour her, at least on this occasion. After all, the box did look rather interesting now Dolita had cleaned it.

"OK," said Hugh, "but I'll come with you. There might be a real treasure in that box and you might try and trick me out of its contents." Enrique laughed, nearly choking on the succulent but grubby looking avocado, which he had just found discarded in a box near one of the market stalls.

"Come on get real," he chortled. "I hardly think there are going to be any fire opals in there and since when did Dolita cheat on anyone?"

"True, true," said Hugh shamefully, giving Dolita a friendly pat on the back.

"Mmm..! Well, I'll go anyway."

Dolita smiled knowing it was most unlikely that Dodgy Deuno would allow Hugh into his precious lock-up.

"Wait," whispered Angelina. "Don't go yet, look what I found. Well actually One-eye found it, just outside the shelter." Her hands were cupped together, held closely to her chest. In them she held what looked like a tiny little mouse. It clearly was frightfully injured and she was not prepared to put it down for One-eye to devour. The others shrugged, most unimpressed, but Dolita like Angelina was not about to see the little thing suffer any more.

"What shall I do with it?" asked Angelina, looking at its cute little face, tiny eyes, small ears and long pointy nose. "I haven't seen a mouse like this before. It's sort of different and so, so cute."

"Well its half dead!" exclaimed Dolita. "Put some water on its nose and put it somewhere safe till I get back. Perhaps if it lives through the next day or so it will be all right."

"Put it where?" asked Angelina with a questioning look on her face.

"I don't know," snapped Dolita abruptly, anxious to find out the contents of the mysterious box. "Put it in one of your handbags it will be safe enough there."

"What a brilliant idea," she said going to find an appropriate bag to make a safe haven for the little animal until Dolita returned from Deuno's. Dolita giggled her usual mischievous giggle. Well! That would certainly keep Angelina busy for the rest of the day, she thought, and off they went.

On foot they weaved through the city congestion. Dodging the infamous green and white cabs, dozens of Volkswagen Beetles, which in their abundance were waiting for the green light at the traffic interchange. Suddenly, foot to the pedal as though it were the race of the century and their life depended on it, off they went to the next set of lights. Their occupants looking bewildered as other cabs, seemingly coming from nowhere, cut across their path. The constant barrage of horns from impatient drivers was rising into the morning air.

This was the city rush hour, everyone who was anyone going to work. A twelve-seater ramshackle old bus turned the corner unexpectedly and Hugh jumped backwards, grabbing hold of Dolita's right arm.

"Ouch," she squealed, "that hurt."

"Tough," he said, "just saved your life," and on they continued. Dolita's heart was now beating faster than ever with anticipation. They left behind the morning frenzy and cut through the quieter back streets towards Dodgy Deuno's lock-up.

When the pair arrived at Deuno's lock-up he was just leaving.

"Deuno, Deuno!" Dolita shouted just in time to stop him disappearing round the corner.

"Hi, what's the urgency?" he inquired.

"This," she said, producing the box from beneath a piece of dirty linen. "I need you to open it." Deuno took the box looking at it inquisitively.

"Nice piece of woodwork, so what is it?"

"That's just it, we don't know," butted in Hugh before Dolita had time to reply.

"Steal it, did you?"

"No," said Dolita, she hesitated, "well sort of, it was left and we found it."

"Looks like something from Oaxaca," said Deuno recognizing the style. He

shrugged his shoulders, winked at Dolita and walked back towards the lock-up. Opening the door and mumbling something about waiting he disappeared into the lockup leaving the door slightly ajar behind him.

Hugh peered curiously round the door. Dolita squeezed beneath him. Neither dared go in uninvited. To go into Dodgy Deuno's lock-up was a truly unique experience, that is, if you could get in, and few people rarely did. Even Martinez was not allowed in, although he left his old taxi there when it was off the road, which was more often than not these days. It was a large lock-up and the previous owners kept in there at least two vehicles and a scooter. No one could actually understand how Dodgy Deuno ever came to have possession of such a lock-up in the first place. Because he was Dodgy I suppose! Sometimes it is better not to ask!

Someone had attempted to paint a vibrant mosaic on the outside wall. Bright purple, shocking pink and pea green shapes were now the remnants of what once might have been considered an interesting piece of art. Graffiti across the mosaic was mostly illegible but for the words 'Molina brothers Rule OK!'

Seemingly the gang used to inhabit this part of town.

"They certainly get around," said Dolita reading the graffiti.

"Who?"

"Them there Molinas" she replied, turning her head to the heavy aluminium double doors which had two locks, three bolts and an additional bolt and chain. A small slim door at the side just allowed sufficient access for one person to squeeze through. This too was heavily locked. A separate wrought-iron wrecker stretched the full length of the garage. For sure, no one was getting in uninvited. The words "Deuno's lockup" were now scrawled in thick black paint across the door. The walls inside had been white-washed but were an array of colours. Damp had seeped through in places causing a growth of both moss and slimy green fungus. In parts, a yellow slime merged with patches of oil on the floor, spilt paint and grease. No one really knew what Deuno kept inside. Dolita who seemed to be the only one who had once had the privilege of going in, said if anything ever existed, Deuno had one. It might not work but he had one: ropes and chains, nuts and bolts, wire and wool, electrical appliances, mechanical appliances, tools and equipment of all manner of description. Everything imaginable hung from the roof. Timbers across the rafters formed storage for more clutter. How he ever found anything in there was a mystery in itself but Deuno seemed to know just where everything was.

"What if there's something valuable in the box and he nicks it?" whispered Hugh.

"Oh, he wouldn't do that," replied Dolita. "You really have a suspicious nature, can't you trust anyone?"

Hugh puzzled, "No! So why wouldn't he? Why do you think he got the name Dodgy Deuno?"

"What's that?" asked Deuno. "Come in if you must but don't touch anything."

Surprised and in his eagerness to enter the mysterious lock-up Hugh accidentally kicked over an aluminium bucket sending it flying. Deuno glared at him. Hugh turned quickly, wacking his head on a tyre hanging from the roof. Dolita couldn't help but giggle.

"*¿Qué onda?*" she said cheekily.

Ignoring her and moving forward to pick up the bucket, whilst rubbing his head he looked worryingly at Deuno.

"Leave it!" Deuno yelled. "There, it's done!" he said, passing the box to Dolita, unlocked but unopened. Dolita looked at Hugh as if to say I told you so and giggled again. "Well go on, open it," urged Deuno.

Dolita was excited wondering what secrets the mysterious box held and she was just about to find out! She opened the box most carefully. Taking out the contents one by one there were three items in all.

A rather spectacular looking red feather, well preserved, with a mottled black fleck running through it.

A charcoal sketch of a girl about 15 or 16 years of age now quite faded and a piece of tatty paper folded into four with the numbers 541342 written on it and the name Helga.

"Is that all?" exclaimed Hugh disappointedly.

"Well," said Deuno. "Suppose they mean something to someone. Come on," he said, ushering them out, "I've got things to do."

Dolita sat on the wall outside the lock-up. Yes, she thought I think they do! Don't know quite what, but I think they do! She stared at the contents. She could see that the sketch was of a fine looking young woman. It was impossible to make out her attire as the sketch was not only faded but it even looked as though at sometime a sticky substance had been spilt on it. She read the numbers again, I wonder who Helga is? Could this be Helga's phone number? Helga's not a Mexican name! Whatever! Dolita knew the number was incomplete because several other digits preceding 541342 were unreadable. The paper was also stained, probably by the same sticky substance that was on the picture.

"Come on," said Hugh. "What you sitting there for? Let's be off." Much ado about nothing if you ask me." He had hoped that after all there would be something exciting in the box, a map leading to some hidden treasure? No, well a few *peso* notes at least!

"You go," urged Dolita, "I'll catch you up."

Poor Dolita! thought Hugh, murmuring to himself as he meandered down the street. "She must be so sad. She really believed there was something special in that box."

The fact was, there was indeed something very special in the box. Dolita was not sure of the significance yet, but something told her that she must take great care of the box, and its contents. Great care!

When they returned to the shelter, Angelina was more interested in her tiny new friend than the contents of the mysterious box. She had hoped they would be more thrilling than some scrappy bits of paper, a useless photo and a feather. Suggesting that Dolita give her the feather to make a bed for her little pet, Dolita was not amused. Meanwhile, Roberto had cracked open a bottle that he'd brought from the house at 247. Had he been able to read, he would have known it said 'Ramon Roqueta Reserva', one of Catalunya's finest wines. He just knew he liked it and swigged it precariously from the broken bottle, the spicy plum aroma filling his nostrils. A big smile on his face, he laughed silently. He too was disillusioned with the contents of the box. What an anticlimax!

CHAPTER 9
RAGGY MAN
TO THE RESCUE

Oh stop that incessant barking," mumbled Roberto.

"How can anyone get any sleep around 'ere? "*¿Qué onda? ¿Qué onda?*" he said pressing his hands to his ears.

"It's 3.30 in the afternoon, you shouldn't be sleeping anyway," said Enrique.

"I think there's something wrong," whispered Dolita, softly.

"With Roberto?" asked Manolo.

"No, *necio*. Raggy Man!"

Everyone knew that Raggy Man could be a pain if he wanted attention, whether it be to tell you he was hungry, or simply wanted to play, Raggy Man was "yappy" at the best of times. He had a lovable temperament and was usually Dolita's constant companion but as she thought about it he had not been around much that day.

"Just where have you been all day Raggy Man?" Dolita asked "and what have you been up to?"

He sat and looked at her, head tilted to one side. He always looked sweet and quite comical when he did this. Today there was such a seriousness about him.

"Yap yap yap," he said shaking his tail furiously.

"Ask Dolita to sort him out," grumbled Roberto. "What does he want?" he asked yawning.

"I don't know," replied Dolita "I think he is trying to tell me something. I think there is something wrong. Show me Raggy what is it? Look he wants me to follow him."

Bozo and One-eye were not around otherwise for sure they would have been joining in the commotion. Certainly when Raggy yapped, Bozo barked, the cat went mad and when the animals started there was no peace for anyone. Raggy kept taking a few steps backwards turning, running towards them and retreating. He was quite excitable and certainly beckoning them.

"Uhm, to play no doubt."

"No this is different, look he wants me to follow him."

"Well there's nothing else to do around here," said Manolo. "Life's been boring since we found the house at 247."

Dolita looked momentarily sad. They never did get the chance to return to the house. One of the older boys, Javier in actual fact, had been in the vicinity a few days later and saw a battered old car and a small white van parked outside. Snooping around a little and crawling through the gap in the bushes he did a quick about turn and got out of there as fast as he possibly could when a rather angry looking large bloke took him by surprise. Hurling abuse at him and waving a rather nasty looking pair of garden shears, Javier scarpered. He had just managed to catch sight of lots of equipment: ladders and various types of building materials.

Dolita sighed at the thought of the house at 247. Shame! They had all wanted to go back! Now it sounded as though it was occupied.

"Come on then, let's follow Raggy, we need a little excitement," said Manolo.

"Angelina, you coming?"

"Yeah of course."

"OK Raggy Man lead the way," shouted Dolita.

"¡*Vamos a ver!*" she called to the others, Angelina and Manolo followed. Raggy quietened down as soon as he realised the others were following him. Roberto went back to sleep.

Of all the street kids Angelina, Manolo and Dolita were the closest. They were good friends and particularly supportive of each other's needs. Angelina used to be quiet, very much in her brother's shadow and walking with him in obedience, though she could often be heard to bicker with him over trivia. Recently she was becoming more independent and assertive. She was beginning to take the lead, much to everyone's astonishment.

"Slow down Raggy you are going too fast!" yelled Dolita, stopping for a moment to catch her breath.

"¿*Qué onda? ¿Qué onda?* Where you kids rushing off to now?" shouted Rosa as they passed swiftly through the market, the kids trying to avoid the chaos as the traders cleared away after the day's business.

"Don't really know but Raggy seems very excited," giggled Dolita.

"Probably found a bone in the *basura*," she laughed, and continued packing away her stall. It was the rainy season and usually at this time the heavens opened; in fact you could almost set your clock by the weather. The dark clouds began to hover overhead looking rather ominous as if to drop their dreary contents at any moment.

Across the *Calle Don Juan*, through the *plaza* and down *Avenida España*, they hurried to keep up with Raggy Man.

"Where on earth are we going and what are you up to Raggy Man? I hope this is not just a wild goose chase," said Dolita, curiously.

"No," smirked Manolo, "it's a wild Raggy chase, he he!"

"Ha ha. Very funny!" replied Dolita.

It was now nearly four in the afternoon.

At least twice the kids stopped and hesitated and wondered whether to continue the chase but when they stopped so did Raggy Man, turning to see if they were still in pursuit.

"Yap yap yap."

"*¡Vale! ¡Vale!* We're coming," cried Dolita, picking up the pace again. "This is strange, he certainly wants to show us something."

By now the wind was blowing furiously and the skies completely clouded over. Fifteen or so minutes into their trail, Manolo shrieked, as they turned the corner. His eyes travelled up and down a narrow overgrown ditch alongside the road.

"*¡Mira! ¡Mira!* Look over there in the *rambla*!" he shouted, pointing to what was clearly a bike overturned and caught up amongst dense bracken and tangled brambles. To the left of the bike was a heap. A familiar looking heap, too true!

"Well, well, well! Just look 'ere!" he said, getting closer to the scene. "It's Mikey Mean, looks like he's come off the bike." Rushing over, Mikey was lying face down but there was no mistaking it was Mikey, even from a distance.

"Do you think he's dead?" asked Angelina, the hairs on the back of her neck standing on end. She shuddered!

"No he's breathing," gasped Dolita, getting closer to him and putting her ear to his face.

"How do you know?"

"Just do," she said and then Mikey moved slightly and groaned.

"Told you so," she whispered smugly.

"Well what do we do now? We can't move him, he is far too heavy and anyway, he might need a *médico*."

"*¡Médico! ¡Médico!* Don't be stupid you *necio*! We're street kids, we don't have a *médico*."

"Well we might have to find one!"

"I know who can help," said Dolita. "The boys from the Crisis Centre, they will know what to do. They always have stuff in their bags.

"Smart thinking, drr… but they are not going to be around at this time of day. You know they always come out in the mornings. Also, it's starting to rain so we are done for."

"Not quite," said Dolita as Raggy yapped. "*¡Mira!* There is Enrique coming down the road on an old lime-green scooter. What a stroke of luck. Flag him down quick Manolo."

"Enrique, stop! What you doing 'ere?"

"Decided to follow you guys and a good thing too I might add. That is one smart dog you have there. Hey Raggy Man you are a star!"

Raggy Man yapped, tilting his head to one side proudly.

"You all right, *botón de oro*?" Dolita grimaced.

"Don't call me buttercup. Yeah, I'm all right," she said, looking at Mikey, "but he isn't!"

"Leave Mikey to me," said Enrique, checking him over. "He's fine, just a small cut to the back of the head and a little concussion. I will get him back to the shelter on the scooter if you can take his bike. Be as quick as you can 'cos this rain is going to come down heavy. If you get caught in it you will be chilled all night."

Suddenly, Raggy nose dived, buckling Dolita's legs and sending her to the ground.

"What on earth is wrong with him now?" asked Manolo, to quickly realise that Raggy had a brightly coloured copperhead in his mouth. Dolita screamed when she became aware of the cold-blooded snake and how near it had been to biting her ankle. Well camouflaged in its surroundings, Mikey also must have had a lucky escape from the snake's strike. With Raggy holding onto the viper for all he was worth, it hissed and struggled, spraying a vile smelling liquid. Quick as lightning, Enrique, seeing the commotion and knowing how to handle such creatures, snatched it from Raggy's grasp, Raggy only too happy to let it go, as Enrique threw it, with great distance, into the *rambla*.

"Right were moving," said Enrique. The others nodded in agreement anxious to get out of the *rambla* without delay. Shuddering, but grateful to Raggy yet again, they were about to clamber out, Dolita's attention then turning to Mikey's bike,

"Actually, speaking of bikes, where is this bike from? Mikey doesn't have a bike," Dolita said to the others looking puzzled.

"Too true, and yeah Enrique, where did you get the scooter?" Manolo asked.

"From Dodgy Deuno of course. Who else would have a scooter like this? It's a vile, pukey colour but it goes. I saw Deuno and I told him something strange was going down. As soon as I mentioned Dolita's name he said I could borrow the scooter. He seems to have a soft spot for you Dolita."

Dolita giggled.

"How come everyone has a soft spot for Dolita?" enquired Manolo.

"You jealous or something?"

"Yeah, a little," he laughed.

"Well don't be. Rosa and the others all pamper her but so they should. After all she's a little treasure and shares everything, so be glad that she's such a good mate and shut up! Now, help me lift Mikey up the banking will you?" Manolo smiled. He too had a soft spot for Dolita. In fact he thought maybe he loved her. Yes why not, he loved her nearly as much as Angelina. No he thought, he loved her more! Angelina after all was a very argumentative sister. He had a groovy kind of love for Dolita. Maybe one day when they were older...?

"What you thinking about Manolo? Come on, give us a hand will you?"

Mikey was heavy, and covered in grunge.

"He smells disgusting," said Manolo, grimacing.

"So what's new?" replied Dolita, giggling. "Trust Mikey to fall in a ditch! Well what was he doing trying to cross the *rambla* anyway?" she said.

Between them they managed to lift him out of the ditch and onto the banking for a further investigation. Enrique carefully checked Mikey over once again. He was by now fully conscious but still quite disorientated. His eyes were rather glazed and he seemed confused about his whereabouts. He also kept mumbling about his arm hurting and feeling sick.

"He probably had a nasty knock on the head but I don't see any serious wounds, just minor cuts and grazes," remarked Enrique.

They lifted him onto the scooter.

"Is his arm broken?" inquired Manolo.

"No don't think so but probably badly sprained."

"Walk with me to the *plaza*," said Enrique. I'll push the scooter, Manolo you and Angelina hold onto Mikey so that he doesn't fall off"

"Yes and I'll bring the bike," said Dolita, though it was far too big for her to ride. "I'll take it to Dodgy Deuno's lock-up. Hopefully he can repair it because the front wheel is all buckled. We can find out who it belongs to later."

Walking slowly and hoping the rain would hold off, they soon reached the *plaza*.

There they separated. Enrique turned left to the shelter, and Angelina accompanied him supporting Mikey on the scooter. Manolo and Dolita turned right towards Dodgy Deuno's. Enrique insisted that Manolo accompany Dolita. He said that from there on he could manage Mikey with Angelina's help. Mikey was now looking much better and the colour had returned to his face though he still seemed to be in a considerable amount of pain with his right arm.

Dolita and Manolo arrived at the lock-up just as the rain came, the faithful little Raggy Man at their side.

"You go to the shelter," she said to Manolo. "I will be fine now."

Manolo hesitated not wanting to leave her but the light shining under Deuno's door suggested he was inside. Deuno would never go out and leave the lights on – he was too thrifty and he knew Dolita would be quite safe with Deuno.

Manolo did not want to hang around unnecessarily as he was not exactly Deuno's favourite person at the moment. Why? Oh, Deuno didn't like many people. He had been surprised to hear that Hugh had managed to get a foot in the precious lock-up when he had taken the mysterious box with Dolita that day. Better wait he thought until Deuno opens the door. He never noticed anyone hanging around in the street nearby.

"Go on," she said, "I'm fine." But he waited patiently.

Dolita pressed the buzzer; there was no answer. Pressing it again she could hear it ringing out. Then, finally movement and shuffling could be heard from inside, the gruff voice of Deuno called out.

"Whooo's there? What yer want?"

"It's me, Dolita. Can I come in? I'm getting wet!"

By now the rain was coming down in torrents and Dolita was pressing her little body against the old aluminium doors of the lock-up to try to get some shelter, feeling the foul discomfort of wet clinging clothes.

The rain sounded angry and the high pitch ringing of drops landing in the broken guttering, empty tin cans and barrels echoed around Deuno's door. Dolita shivered, Raggy Man was dishevelled and Deuno looked through the spyhole that he had made in the door: he couldn't see anyone! Well of course he wouldn't see anyone. Little Dolita was only 3 feet, 5 inches tall and the spyhole was well above her height.

"Let me in," she pleaded and then to her relief she heard the sound of the bolts, as one by one Deuno pulled them across, opening the door to let her enter. At that point Manolo winked, patted her on the shoulder and with a backward glance, took off at high speed back to the shelter.

CHAPTER 10
EARLY NEXT MORNING

When Dolita finally emerged from Dodgy Deuno's she virtually collided with a guy hovering outside. He was hanging around in the doorway behaving in a very shifty manner. The pair startled each other, and ordinarily she would have ignored him and carried on her way but she caught sight of Maria Molina across the street and decided to wait around until she had moved on.

Dolita used the moment to chat to the stranger.

Maria Molina was not the girl's real name but as she had been known to associate with the Molina brothers for such a long time they seemed to have adopted her. Maria was particularly close to Pablo Molina. Unfortunately to Dolita's detriment Maria had witnessed her and Manolo wheel the bike down to Dodgy Deuno's lock-up, she was sure that it was Pablo's bike, although when she had last seen Pablo the previous night, he had not mentioned that it was missing. Maria had watched as Manolo left Dolita at Deuno's and was just about to challenge her as Deuno opened the door and let her in, of course taking the bike with her. Maria decided to stick around and unfortunately for her that meant all night, because Dolita did not reappear until the next morning. Much to her annoyance Bobby Sniff also turned up and decided to crash out in Deuno's doorway.

It had been an awful night; it was as though the Heavens opened, this being the reason that prompted Dolita to stay at Deuno's till next morning.

"May as well crash 'ere," Deuno had said, "you're safe and dry at least," and he showed her a cosy corner with plenty of warm blankets and squidgy cushions. She had wriggled out of her soaking wet clothes into a large black-brushed cotton shirt, one of Deuno's. Looking absolutely ridiculous but not quite as daft as she had looked in Beeky's oversized blouse she didn't care. It was better to be warm and dry, and for that she was grateful.

"I'll be working all night, got something to fix by morning. Got stuff to do, then I'll look at this 'ere bike and you can tell me how you came by it," said Deuno. "So, I'll leave you to it then, Raggy's all right I suppose!" he sniggered, giving Raggy a friendly clip across the ear. Dolita smiled, nodded and settled down for the night.

As you can imagine the next morning Maria was in a foul mood, cold, wet and tired. She was determined to find out what Dolita was up to and if she indeed had Pablo's bike and why, consequently she had stayed in the doorway across the street.

Having had little or no shelter, the prevailing wind and rain had battered her incessantly all night, but Maria waited, she knew the rewards would be worth it. Anything to keep her in favour with the Molinas. If Pablo's bike was stolen and she recovered it she would be their hero, well heroine to be precise.

Maria watched Dolita speaking to Bobby Sniff, she saw her glance across the street in her direction and she caught her expression. Blast…! The young

Dolita had seen her. She had no alternative but to move on, so as not to arouse further suspicion. She knew only too well which route Dolita would take from there. Maria had seen Dolita before and knew that she stayed with the kids behind the metro. She decided to lie in wait for her in the next *calle* and moved on.

Consequently, it was early the next morning and

Maria

Dolita was on her way back to the shelter, without the bike, which she had left with Deuno for repair. She had now forgotten about Maria and was thinking about the tall, skinny guy that she had met in Deuno's doorway. She was thinking how empty his eyes were, vacant and expressionless when suddenly... A swift jolt from behind and Dolita found herself on the floor. Before she realized what was happening Maria Molina had her by the hair and with all the weight of her chubby body she had her pinned to the ground.

The startled Dolita did not have the slightest idea what prompted the attack and she certainly couldn't make out what Maria was saying, who was too angry and incoherent to make any real sense. Dolita was afraid. She knew that she was no match for Maria even though she herself had been known to throw a good punch when the situation demanded it.

Wondering how she was going to escape from this awful dilemma she decided to scream as loud as her lungs would allow. What she did not expect was her "knight in shining armour" to appear so quickly, least of all it to be him. The one they called Bobby Sniff.

With a swift hand movement Maria was being pulled off the grateful Dolita and hurled aside. Raggy Man wanting to show his support ran towards her and nipped her hard on the ankle. She squealed. There, thought Raggy, that will teach you! Wishing he had done that sooner. Maria hissed angrily and scarpered before Raggy decided to go for the other ankle.

Dolita sighed with relief.

"Wow! That was close. Thanks guys. Don't know what all that was about but thanks anyway."

It was quite an eventful time for Raggy. This was the third time he had come to the rescue. He had led them to Mikey, stopped the dreaded viper and now this. As for Bobby… he had played his part too, but Raggy had really come to the rescue, nipping Maria hard. Raggy felt very proud.

* * *

As for Bobby and Dolita it was the beginning of a friendship. A friendship in part because Bobby's head was so messed up he found it hard to form any kind of real relationship.

Bobby decided to hang around for a while. He wanted to make sure that Maria didn't return. He walked with Dolita as far as the metro and then he knew she was on home ground and quite safe. They saw Miggy in the distance just getting ready to go shoe shining. Enrique was cleaning the insipid, pukey looking lime-green scooter. Miggy and Enrique didn't sleep late, like the others, and were always up and about early.

"Thanks Bobby, want to come and meet the other *chavos*?" said Dolita.

Bobby took a deep breath and sniffed with such fervour it sounded as though his whole insides were

being sucked upwards, from the tip of his toes to the top of his head. Dolita squirmed and wrinkled her face, "er disgusting." Then, glancing down at his feet, she saw he had odd tennis shoes. Amazing she had not noticed that before but I suppose it's hardly surprising. After all it had been an eventful few hours.

Giggling and now content in the reassurance she was on home ground, she nodded as Bobby sniffed again and signalled he was going. Ever grateful to him, she wondered what he was really like. He was skinny that was for sure.

Very tall and very skinny. His eyes were strange, yes she thought empty, she had noticed earlier, so empty. Feeling she would see him again she smiled and nodded, she certainly owed him a favour.

"Hi, mi *botón de oro pequeña*," said Enrique "you OK and who was that?"

"Oh it's a long story."

"So I'm listening," he whispered.

"OK, but first tell me about Mikey. How is he?"

"Oh he's fine. A few bruises and probably a sprained wrist but he will be OK, just won't be using his wrist for a few days. He needs to rest his arm. Now tell me what Deuno said about the bike, and who was that tall lanky guy? I wondered whom the bike belonged to. Mikey told me that he just saw it propped up against a wall and there was nobody around. Hard to believe 'cos it looked a mean machine to me and I bet it's worth a bob or two."

Dolita puzzled and then sitting herself down on the banking, while Enrique finished cleaning the scooter, she told him the tale about Maria Molina and her knight in shining armour.

* * *

Interestingly enough it was indeed Dolita's turn to help Bobby a few days later. She saw him sleeping in a doorway, disorientated and just about to take a cigarette from a rather nasty looking fat guy. Dolita waded in and distracted him suspecting it would be no ordinary cigarette and probably laced with something. As indeed it was! The *Padrote* lingered and then idly strolled away.

Maybe Dolita had just saved Bobby's life! Now they were even, a favour for a favour.

Later the next day it was Bozo's turn to cause a commotion. Most of the kids were sleeping, settled down for a few hours' kip; Raggy Man was out for the count. He was well and truly snuggled under Dolita's blanket. Suddenly, Bozo went barmy, charging about hurtling from mattress to mattress.

Angelina screeched as he jumped on her stomach before throwing himself around in a 90-degree turn, nearly nosediving on her little purple satin bag and splatting her new tiny pet. Apart from Roberto who slept on, everyone was soon on their feet in horror. Raggy Man awakened, he didn't know why, he didn't know what was up, but he didn't need an excuse to bark. If Bozo was excited about something, then he would be excited too! Following Bozo's lead this looked like fun. He ran over to the water barrel and bashed it with such force it's contents went everywhere.Next Roberto was awake, right in the firing line; the cold murky water covered him from top to toe.

"What the heck was that?" he shouted, shuddering as the cold water cascaded all over him. Suddenly Bozo headed straight for him, dived across his body leaving mucky paw prints on his beige fleecy sweater and charged back in the direction of Angelina who was now safe, guarding herself and her little pet from another pounce. It was like a whirlwind and nobody could seem to make any sense of what was happening until Rocia, taking control screamed out

"*¡Mira! ¡Mira! ¡Ratas!*" Not a rat, no, not a rat but rats.

A colony of the things, well maybe not a colony but certainly too many for comfort.

"Passing through?!" cried Rocia, hands on heavy hips, eyeballing one of the creatures. "Well better be," she screamed "'cos you're not settling 'ere you dirty little rodents," she screeched, picking up a wooden stake.

"Where did they come from?" mumbled the sleepy and now very wet Roberto.

"Get 'em boys" shouted Rocia as Bozo and Raggy Man set to work ridding the shelter of the unwanted guests. By the time One-eye turned up everything was back under control. Sadly for him, he had missed all the fun!

"It doesn't make sense" exclaimed Rocia, "We expect the occasional rat but why so many of them?"

"Doesn't bear thinking about" whimpered Dolita, who was very sweetly trying to find Roberto some dry clothes and was determined to sleep under two blankets in future, making sure none of her bodily parts protruded.

"You know," said Enrique chatting to Dolita later. "I don't know what we would do without our animals."

Bozo and Raggy Man stood proudly side-by-side, Bozo towering over Raggy, One-eye looked on.

Angelina's little friend was safely tucked away in its handbag, nowhere to be seen.

(HAPTER 11
MIKEY AND THE
STOLEN BIKE

A new day and Rocia was washing. Angelina decided to tidy the shelter after the mayhem caused by the rats the day before and some of the kids were still sleeping, oblivious to the activities around them. Angelina had her pictures hanging proudly on the wall near her corner of the mattress and had been examining her collection of bags, which now amounted to about 10 in all, of varying styles, shapes and colours. Not forgetting the one of course that she had given to her tiny new friend! One dainty, red satin bag looked as though it had never been used. It was adorned in diamante beading and was still stuffed with white tissue paper keeping it perfectly in shape. Putting them all away safely having finished her chores she sighed, it was a perfect day, she wandered over to talk to Rocia.

"How do you manage to get things so clean?" Angelina asked.

"Hard work and tons of scrubbin'," said Rocia in a muffled voice, chewing on a piece of liquorice and rubbing a white T-shirt for all she was worth. She had it immersed in cold water in an old kitchen sink: one that they had salvaged from the *basura*.

She then hung the shirt on a makeshift line: namely, a piece of dirty rope straggled from a rusty nail in the shelter wall, stretched across to the branches of a nearby tree. The washing blew gently in the breeze and an oversized, grossly fat, ugly-looking lizard scuttled across the ground and shot up the trunk of the tree. Camouflaged well in a God-given suit to aid his survival, he disappeared into the branches. Rocia ignored it and carried on with the next item of clothing. Angelina gave a half smile and sauntered off.

A card game was beginning to get out of hand as a group of half a dozen *chavos* and *chavas* turned over an old milk crate and utilized it as a table, the centerpiece for their game. Someone had come by a fresh croissant, it was still warm and they passed it around sharing it until Mikey snatched the remainder and wolfed it down. Hugh shared a packet of *chicle*.

Five minutes later: "Stop cheating!" screamed Dolita prodding Mikey in the ribs.

Mikey looked awkward and frowned having been found out.

"How do you know I've been cheating?" he asked.

"Just do," she screamed. "Why are you always so mean? You spoil everything."

"Stop cheating, *¡Chapusero! ¡Chapusero!* she shrieked again when he continued his devious antics, this time she prodded him harder on the right arm.

"Hey Dolita, that's my bad arm."

Mikey stomped off slamming his hand of cards down on the makeshift table.

"Oh, didn't mean to do that," said Dolita apologetically remembering that his arm was still giving him some jip since he fell off the bike into the *rambla*.

"Well it's his own fault," hissed one of the other boys "I'm sick of him cheating."

"Yeah," cheered another of the *chavos*, ignoring Mikey's tantrum, spitting his *chicle* as far as he could and nodding, seemingly pleased with his effort, he carried on with the game. "Good hand, good hand." "Yeah," he shouted again." It's a win. It's a win," and he proudly threw all his cards down with great excitement. The others cheered; actually they made quite a racket. Roberto stirred. "Shush trying to sleep" he mumbled.

"So what's new?" laughed Angelina. "There's something wrong with that *chavo*. No one should sleep this much!"

"It's boredom," replied Alejandro who had now arrived at the shelter and joined them for a game.

"That and the drugs of course."

Dolita looked towards Roberto with sadness in her eyes. She was worried about Roberto. So too were Alejandro and Daveed.

Alejandro and Daveed were part of a Street Crisis team. They visited the kids as often as they could, at least once a week, usually Thursdays. The problem was the huge numbers of *chavos* living on the streets and the Crisis teams could only reach a few of them. Not enough workers, not enough money was Alejandro's complaint.

"Still, we do what we can," he said and so they did. Alejandro and Daveed had dedicated their lives to helping the street kids. When a local reporter for the city news asked, "What difference can you make, there are so many *chavos* on the streets?" Alejandro replied with this wonderful analogy.

"Thousands of turtles are washed up by the tide each year. Left on the beach in the midday sun they die. What difference would it make if you had a little time to spare and you threw a few back into the sea?"

"It would make a huge difference to the ones you threw back," said the reporter.

"Well there you have your answer," Alejandro replied.

"We do what we can!"

The street kids so looked forward to the visits from the Crisis team. The highlight of the week was a game of cards. Oh and *fútbol*, of course. Yeah, that's what the Spanish-speaking people call it, *fútbol*. Alejandro and Daveed tried to visit the kids on the same day each week to introduce some routine into their lives. They also tried to encourage the kids to visit the Crisis Centre. At least there they could have a hot meal, enjoy the facilities to wash their clothes and take a hot shower. The Crisis Centre also had a resident doctor and dentist. The problem being it was the far side of the city. Too far to walk and naturally it cost money to take the metro or an *autobús*. Something street kids didn't have.

Enrique had gone to stay there for a few weeks earlier in the year. He had helped in the kitchen. This is of course where he had learnt his few words of English.

Alejandro was worried about all the kids but he was especially concerned about Roberto.

Roberto was sniffing glue, a very dangerous thing to do but unfortunately not uncommon on the streets. The sad fact was Roberto thought it would solve his problems, at least make them go away. In fact the reverse was true. Things were getting worse and Alejandro knew it.

Alejandro tried on numerous occasions to persuade Roberto to go with them to the Centre for a few days, but without success. He was having none of it. Dolita was particularly worried about Roberto because she had seen the damaging effects that glue sniffing had upon some of the other *chavos*. She could not bear the thought of dear Roberto going the same way.

The game over, the kids dispersed and Alejandro pulled up another old abandoned milk crate, turned it upside down and sat on it to talk to Dolita. She loved to sit and talk with him, she learnt so much from him.

He often had interesting things stashed in his holdall that he eagerly brought to show her. Today was no exception.

"Look at this," he said, taking a small square box with a glass cover, out of his bag.

"It's a Monarch!"

Dolita wrinkled her brow and took a closer look.

"What? Looks like a *mariposa*, to me."

Alejandro smiled, "Yes, a *mariposa*, but a very special one. A Monarch Butterfly."

"Mmm! It's very beautiful, said Dolita.

"Monarch butterflies are one of the most glorious

and beautiful of the millions of insects who migrate across great distances in the course of their lives. Their life and migration pattern is one of the most complex of any," explained Alejandro.

"How do you know such stuff? Tell me more" she said, reaching out to see the butterfly again, chuffed that he had brought it to show her, carefully preserved in its small glass case. Roberto who heard part of the conversation looked puzzled and mumbled to himself.

"Well that's a load of useless information if ever I heard any," he said, and turned away pulling his sweater over his head, he went back to sleep.

Alejandro continued unperturbed.

"Their migration pattern," he went on, "is more complex than that of most other birds, fish or insects. There are four generations of butterflies in the course of a year. The first three generations only live up to six weeks from the time they develop out of the caterpillar stage until death. These three separate generations live their short lives in Canada during the spring and summer months. The fourth generation, which includes hundreds of millions of Monarchs, migrates from Canada."

"Where's Canada?" she asked curiously.

"Three thousand miles north from the mountainous plateaus here in Mexico."

Dolita frowned, "Sounds a long way to me!"

"Sure is, and they survive on water alone for no less than four months from December and then begin to feed on the abundance of nectar from the flowers building massive fuel reserves ready for their 3,000 miles return journey back. They mate and on March

21st each year, the enormous colony of millions of Monarch butterflies ascends from its Mexico home to begin the epic migration back. The Monarchs, on return, then give birth to the next generation and the whole process begins again."

"How do they know to go back on the same day each year?" Dolita asked. Alejandro caught her puzzled expression.

"One of life's little miracles," he replied. "One of the many mysteries of God's creation I think." He smiled and gave her a loving glance.

"*¡Qué lindo! ¡Qué lindo!*" she said. "It is so beautiful.

I would love to see it fly."

"Well not much chance of that," he laughed, placing it back in his bag so carefully and looking at his watch to check the time.

Angelina who had listened to some of the discussion about the butterflies was now more than anxious to introduce Alejandro to her little friend.

He was not in a glass case! He was not dead! She very proudly produced her purple satin handbag, and he was very much alive. The little mouse who was now regaining his strength and whose wounds seemed to be healing naturally had become very precious to her. It was most certainly her tender loving care and patience that had orchestrated his survival.

One-eye, who had kept his eye on the little fella, was sure that without a doubt, if he touched, he would be in big, big trouble, with Angelina.

"Wow," said Alejandro as he took hold of the little creature. "He sure is a cutey, looks like a little shrew with his long pointy nose, but I suspect he is a Mexican pygmy mouse."

"Ah! I wondered what to call him," exclaimed Angelina, stroking his dense velvety fur as she gently replaced him in the bag. "I will call him Pygmy," she said dropping a few bits of vegetation into the bottom of the bag and watching as he gritted his sharp red teeth in gratitude.

"Did you learn about the butterflies at school when you were younger Alejandro?" enquired Dolita, once again turning the topic of conversation to the butterflies.

"University actually. I intended to study botany and wildlife but after a few months I left the course, couldn't put my mind to it. I had a mate who worked in the Probation Department. He introduced me to some of the kids he was working with. They weren't bad kids, just seemed to have lost their way a bit. Before I knew it I was hooked and I did some voluntary work in an area they call the Bronx. Later I went back to university to study psychology."

"What's psychology?"

He laughed. "How the mind works. I learnt how to understand kids and look after such as you lot!" He laughed again with a glint in his eye. "Quite a change from butterflies, eh? These kids on the Bronx really touched my heart."

"Tell me about them. What is the Bronx like? Do they live on the streets?"

"Sure do, though we don't call them *chavos* in the Bronx. That's a Mexican term."

Well Alejandro didn't have time to continue his story because suddenly there was a great disturbance.

CHAPTER 12
THE RUMBLE

"Rumble, scrap, rumble!" shouted one of the kids and everyone jumped to their feet.

"Where?"

"Near the Rumba bar."

"Where?"

"Corner of Don Jose, behind *Café Casa Azul*. It's serious stuff."

"I know where it is," said Dolita who knew every back street and café bar in that part of town, "I will show you."

"OK, we're on our way," said Manolo.

Alejandro picked up his bag in which he always had a variety of items for occasions such as this, he and Daveed were ready to go with them. Complete with plasters, bandages and First Aid stuff.

"Come on move it," shouted one of the other boys. "*¡Vamos a ver!*" No one missed 'a good fight'.

"Bum," said Dolita. "*¡Chavos!* What's wrong with them? The least excuse for a fight!" She didn't know the reason behind the fight but someone yelled that Mikey Mean was involved.

Everywhere Mikey went, trouble went. His attitude rubbed everyone up the wrong way, he certainly had a real chip on his shoulder. Dolita later found out that the fight had broken out because he had taken the bike.

"I knew it, I knew it! I knew there would be trouble over that wretched bike!" she exclaimed wondering how Mikey had gone from playing cards with her only a few minutes earlier to getting embroiled in a fight the next. She knew he had stomped off in a bad mood, but thought that he was hanging around the shelter not three blocks away.

Pow! Wallop! Ugh!

"Pack it in now," yelled Alejandro wading in to separate the boys. Alejandro turned suddenly, Daveed standing in the wrong place at the wrong time took a punch to the right cheek.

He felt his face smart.

"Wow! Some of these youngsters can really throw a punch" he said, as someone shouted, "Get out of the way *gringo*, this has nothing to do with you," and suddenly he was pushed aside as a lad came lunging forward to take another punch at Mikey.

Mikey had given little thought to his already injured arm. He had been too busy defending himself from what appeared to be a very angry and hostile guy.

"Kick him where it hurts," came the voice of an onlooker.

Dolita to the rescue ran across and put out her left leg just at the right moment to send the lad hurtling to the ground.

"Nice one Dolita," shouted another of the kids in the crowd, which was now gathering and encircling the fight.

Fight! Fight! came the chants, but by now Daveed had Mikey firmly in his grasp and Alejandro was holding the other lad tightly, until he promised a truce. Mikey shrugged and dusted himself down as Daveed released him. Suddenly before anyone realised what was happening the fight broke out again.

"Come on *chavos*," came a cry. This time they came from nowhere. Alejandro and Daveed knew when to back off and let the kids sort out their differences. It was now a gang fight. The shelter kids versus the Molina brothers. Yes, where on earth had they come from? News on the streets had been they had moved to the other side of town. The Molina brothers were bad news.

"I don't believe it," Dolita cried out, "Only Mikey could take a bike belonging to one of the Molina brothers."

Yes, Mikey found the bike looking abandoned, took it and did a runner! In his haste, trying to take a short cut across the *rambla*, he fell off the thing, ending up in the ditch as well you know.

It could only happen to Mikey! Well more to the point, worse than that, Dolita had it now! The Molina brothers would never believe that she had not been party to this. They would never believe that she had not intended to keep it.

Mikey had taken Pablo Molina's bike. Dolita was now beginning to see the connection. Of course, Maria Molina must have seen her with Pablo's bike at Deuno's lock-up, which explained everything. She obviously thought she was involved in the theft. Now what?

"Cheers Mikey," she muttered sarcastically under her breath. "Thanks a million!"

The chanting increased, other kids all suddenly finding themselves in the brawl, blows to the head, shouting and swearing. Bodies everywhere, it was difficult to see who was fighting whom.

Dolita's voice, "Leave it out, stop it!" could barely be heard, smothered by the shouts and cries of the fighters.

"This stinks!" cried Dolita, who hated to see anyone hurt.

Pablo Molina was the youngest of the brothers, but he was a tough brawny character. He was furious and charged at Mikey with an angry animalistic expression on his face, the sheer weight of his body against Mikey's slim frame threw him to the ground. Before the startled Mikey could react he was pinned down. Pablo straddled across him with his knees pressed against his shoulders. Mikey was well and truly pinned down, now he couldn't do a thing. Dolita turned and there she was, Maria Molina hurtling towards her in frenzy. With a sigh of exasperation she spun round and looked for Alejandro, only to see the local *policía* coming round the corner. What perfect timing.

The noise of the siren and the screech of the brakes, the street emptied.

Rumble, what rumble?

It ended as quickly as it had begun. The street was left empty all but for a few stragglers. Dolita, Alejandro and Daveed looked at one another, bemused.

"I'm out of here," shouted Dolita and like a streak of lightning, she too was gone.

Alejandro and Daveed were left to explain the fiasco.

"That was so stupid" said Dolita to Mikey Mean back at the shelter. She felt sick, a mixture of anger and despair. "This has got to stop. Fighting's not the way.

"Oh, shut up Dolita," he said, wiping his bruised face with a dirty rag revealing a mixture of blood, dirt and snot. Looking down at his torn jeans he snivelled.

"Do you think I started it? Well no, as a matter of fact I didn't." "No, but you took the bike. It was obvious that it belonged to someone.

No one leaves a smart bike like that. What prompted you to be so stupid?"

"There was no one about, the bike was just there, I thought it was abandoned."

"Mikey Mean, I think you knew very well what you were doing. You stole it thinking you could get away with it. It's just your luck that it belonged to Pablo Molina and someone saw you take it. "Mikey listen to me, I… "

"¡*Cállate!* Shut up! I know, little Miss Dolita, always right. I know, I know," and he half stumbled and walked off to sit alone, his head cupped in his hands.

Dolita was a smart kid; everyone's friend and she so wanted to help Mikey Mean. She decided to let the subject drop; at least for a while. Mikey was always getting into fights and this latest episode was one too many. She decided to talk to Old Ma Kensie. She would know what to do. One thing for sure, they had to get the bike from Dodgy Deuno's lock-up and return it to Pablo Molina before there was more trouble.

The last thing they wanted was gang warfare.

Alejandro and Daveed had gone, having first got rid of the Police presence, who had bigger fish to fry. Most of the kids were settled down in the shelter for the night: no one felt like venturing out in case trouble kicked off again.

Early the next morning Dolita took off with Raggy Man to see Ma Kensie. By now news was out on the streets, Mikey had a wanted sign on his head and strangely enough so did Dolita. Dolita began to think this was weird. It was only a bike after all.

Dolita found Ma Kensie huddled in the doorway of the *Oficina de Ventas* and Ma Kensie listened to Dolita's tale about the fight with Maria Molina and then with the other *chavos*. She was smart and knew everything about everything; she certainly knew the tricks of the Molina brothers.

"They are going to grow up just like their grandfather. No good he was, doing time somewhere in the southern state and those young Molinas are heading for the same fate if someone doesn't take hold of them," she said.

Dolita listened intently.

She didn't know much about the Molinas, other than their name seemed to keep cropping up on the streets and Pablo was the youngest of the bunch.

"Check the handlebars," Ma Kensie whispered to Dolita, "then set up a meeting with Toni and Andre Molina, Hugh and Enrique. Tell them it was all a big mistake and that if they promise not to harm Mikey, or any of the other shelter kids including yourself, you will have the bike returned to them within 24 hours. Arrange mutual ground as a meeting place, and you take the bike Dolita. I know these guys; mean as they appear they are not going to hurt you. As for Maria Molina, well they will sort her out, too."

"Yeah right," said Dolita, shrugging her shoulders and jumping to her feet. Too right they would do a deal, a truce for the bike.

"Oh, and by the way" said Ma Kensie, "don't be too hard on Mikey. His head is messed up. He could do with a little affection; he's been hurt so badly in the past, he doesn't know how to love. You see his emotions have shut down and all he knows is what he saw as a young child: beaten, abused, neglected, and unloved by an angry mother and a drunken stepfather. All he understands is anger, suppose that's why he gets into so many fights. He was deeply traumatised when he saw his little sister killed in a road traffic accident, left him bitter and angry."

"Oh jeeps, how terrible!" exclaimed Dolita, "I had no idea! How come you know so much?"

"Oh, not much I don't know about what goes on around 'ere," she replied.

She gave Ma Kensie a hug and set off to find Enrique and Hugh. As she recited Ma Kensie's plan to them she suddenly remembered her words, "check the handlebars." What could she mean?

Hugh put word out on the streets to set up the meeting, while Enrique and Dolita went to see Deuno to arrange the collection of the bike.

"Good as new," said Deuno, looking at the bike, which certainly was most excellent. With its light aluminium frame the bike was built for speedy urban riding. A 24-speed gear system, in velvet black paint and with beefy handlebars, it combined the best of a mountain bike, a tourer and a roadster

"The wheel was buckled and a flat tyre, but all sorted," Deuno said. "Oh, except for the handlebars, they're a little loose. I'll tighten them."

"No, wait a minute," said Enrique, "let me see." Sure enough the handlebars did need tightening. "Can you get these off?" he asked.

"Are you crazy? I'm supposed to be repairing the bike, not dismantling it."

"It's important," said Enrique. "Just humour me. You can soon put it back together." Deuno was now beginning to get the picture. Dolita looked puzzled.

Deuno took his wrench and with a few swift movements of his hand and a little pressure the handlebars were free.

"Look inside," said Enrique. Dolita peered over Deuno's shoulder as he pulled out a small packet containing white powder. Taking a thin piece of wire he then extracted several more. Enrique opened a packet and sniffed it, "Wow, this is worth a fortune on the streets. Hard stuff. No wonder there was such a fuss over this 'ere bike. Put it back Deuno, the bike's going."

Deuno looked, a questioning expression on his face. "Wow!" He exclaimed, "If these handlebars are stuffed, the chances are the main frame is too! This is one bike I'm not letting go of!"

"Deuno, the bike's going, stuffed handlebars and all. Do you want to see your lock-up set aflame 'cos if you keep this stuff it will be more trouble than it's worth."

Dolita agreed. "Yeah, get rid of it, too right." She knew that this was something she didn't want to be involved in.

The bike again intact, the secret of the handlebars was once more a secret, but off they went to meet with the Molinas, leaving behind Deuno with a disappointed expression on his face.

"Let me do the talking," said Enrique.

"But… but Ma Kensie said…"

"Listen, *mi botón de oro pequeña*, leave this to me," he insisted.

"Right-oh," she grumbled, "but don't call me that. Ugh! I hate it when you call me buttercup."

Enrique smiled his usual smouldering look. If there was one person who could make her do as she was told it was Enrique and he knew it.

"*¡Vale! ¡Vale!*" she said and they walked in the direction of the shelter to collect Hugh.

The rendezvous was near the *Café Casa Azul*, not far from where the fight had broken out. Toni and Andre Molina looked mean, Dolita saw Pablo hovering in the background.

I bet Pablo has no idea what is in the handlebars of that bike, or what other secrets it might hold, she thought.

Uhm ….well! Dolita kept her mouth shut and left it to the guys, who struck a deal after a long conversation and a few raised voices. The bike was handed over and Dolita just prayed that the Molinas kept their side of the bargain. She and Mikey were off the hook, what a relief.

This turned out to be another of those ever eventful dramas in the life of Dolita that she could do without.

114

The three of them walked home, Raggy Man following close by Dolita's side.

Looking up at Enrique and Hugh, one either side both overshadowing her with their height and stature she smiled, giggled her infamous giggle and on they went to live another day.

CHAPTER 13
CHARLOTTE'S QUEST

Alejandro arrived at the office early. He threw open the door, the room smelt musty. Daveed and Maria were late, especially Maria, who had never been particularly good at timekeeping.

At least Daveed could have a coffee and some quiet time, make a start on the mound of paperwork overshadowing his desk, before the others arrived. There was hardly room for him in the office and sharing it with Daveed and Maria was an absolute nightmare. He was hankering for the day when the renovations would be finished in the rest of the building and he could claim his 'space' back. Clambering over the mass of clutter he threw his overstuffed duffle bag and thin, nylon, grey coat in the far corner of the room and waded over to the small rectangular table which housed the kettle, coffee pot and other needy supplies. Flicking the switch he strolled across to his desk, sitting down with an enormous sigh and wondering where to begin. The kettle made some awful grating sound.

"Oh blast!" he muttered. He really should remember to check the water level!

Three cups of coffee later, not having made much impact on the paperwork, the others came trundling in.

"Meeting in the *Director*'s office, 10 minutes," exclaimed Daveed, "some visitor to the project wants showing around."

"*¡Vale!*" said Alejandro, glancing upwards as Daveed strolled towards the kettle, threw the switch checking the water level and mumbling something about the milk being sour, then disappearing out of the office to find some more.

"Strange" thought Alejandro, "it tasted fine to me!"

"How's the leg?" Alejandro asked Maria, looking at her sympathetically. She was wearing a very elegant pair of black trousers, which gave nothing away. Maria always did look immaculate, but it was easy for her, confined to office duties, unlike himself and Daveed who often found themselves out on the streets at a moment's notice.

Maria grimaced, "Not good Alejandro, another course of antibiotics and I need to see the *medico* again."

Alejandro frowned. "Eeek! *¡Lo siento!*

During the building renovations floors had been lifted and dividing walls demolished. The building was well past its best and they should have moved out a long time ago. Unfortunately there was nowhere else that was affordable and sufficient enough to meet their needs.

A large dustsheet separated the main office block from the building work. Something had crawled out from the foundations, 'thing' being the operative word: disturbed in its natural habitat; Maria felt it bite. Now the *médicos* were trying to discover the identity of the mystery biter and how to counteract the venom that it had injected into her left calf muscle. The flesh of the inflamed tissue was slowly being eaten away and what originally looked like a tiny pinprick was now oozing liquid and resembled an ulcer, with a 2cm diameter.

"The *Director*'s waiting," said Daveed popping his head around the door, tutting and rolling his eyes because he had not had time to make a cuppa.

"Two minutes," said Alejandro picking up his notepad, gold-rim glasses and pen. A cheeky wink and pat on the shoulder for Maria, he was out of there.

"This is Charlotte," said the *Director* introducing her to the guys. "Over from England for a few weeks. She wants to see how we work. Any chance of you guys taking her out on the streets for a couple of days?"

"Sure, no problem," said Alejandro, smiling, "as long as you know the risks out there."

Charlotte nodded; she had been briefed!

"Well, no time like the present," the *Director* said. "I will get someone to show Charlotte around the project and make a few security arrangements while you guys sort yourselves out, let's meet in the foyer in one hour."

"Bum! What a pain," said Alejandro, returning to the office, "bang goes my paperwork day"

"Oops!" exclaimed Maria, making her favourite drink of Twinings Raspberry and Echinacea tea, putting her nose in the cup to savour the aroma.

"Yeah, you might well say oops," said Alejandro sarcastically, "I have tons of correspondence to deal with and I haven't checked my e-mails for days. I can't do two things at once!"

"You could if you were a woman," said Maria fluttering her long, captivating eyelashes.

"Watch it!" he said, laughing. "I'll pray that God slows down time."

Alejandro, a charismatic believer, raised his hands to the heavens and rested them on his chest.

"See what I can get done in the next hour," he said. "Don't talk to me." He sat at his old, battered desk, shifting about the papers and switched on his very excellent computer, donated by one of the sponsors of the project.

"Yes, Sir," said Maria, saluting and chuckling at the same time.

* * *

Charlotte's tour around the centre was interesting. A few paid helpers; many of the workers were volunteers.

The Crisis Centre had facilities for 100 kids at any given time: equal numbers of dormitories for boys and girls, segregated of course. Facilities for "drop in", hot showers and laundry amenities, soup kitchens and a visiting dentist and *médico*.

An AIDS-awareness course was running in the main schoolroom, with a group of about 12 in attendance. Charlotte soon learned some of the street language and that the kids called themselves *chavos* and *chava*s on the streets. The Crisis Centre was a hive of activity.

The Motto *'La calle no es lugar para un niño'* ('The street is no place for a kid') was inscribed above the main foyer entrance. A large courtyard was central to the complex and a small group of kids played *fútbol* only too eager to postpone the game to meet their new visitor from England. It was hard to tell the boys from the girls, all femininity as usual hidden behind jogging bottoms, baggy tops and baseball caps. After her tour of the Centre, Charlotte flanked by Daveed and Alejandro was heading for the streets. She wore plain grey combat pants, a T-shirt and linen waistcoat, tennis shoes and baseball cap. Carrying a thin, lightweight calf-length rain mac, it being the rainy season, she felt drab enough not to get noticed. A small black linen shoulder bag housed a few contents, tissues and other possible essentials. What little money she had, was safely housed in her trouser pocket, well secured with two buttons and a flap.

The security guard closed the tall iron gates to the Crisis Centre and the three of them walked towards the *plaza*, proceeding to the end of the *calle* and down the nearest subway to the metro. Charlotte hated the metro. Several years travelling on the London Underground in the rush hour was enough to last her a lifetime. Now here she was on the Mexican City metro but she was not about to let her new companions Alejandro and Daveed see her discomfort. The pair were to become her constant companions for the next two days, one flanking her to the right the other to the left. Ducking and diving, shifting from metro to *autobús*, they visited various kids in their habitat in different parts of the city. A brother and sister sleeping rough in a shop doorway. A group of *chavos* hanging about near the drug store. Some refusing to be disturbed submerged under a pile of dirty blankets and shredded newspaper, suffering the consequences of alcohol and drug abuse from the night before. A few *chavos* sheltering in an old, abandoned transit van at the entrance to the park and finally those who she found to be most fascinating.

"A group of about fifteen live here," said Alejandro, "the girls are not here at the moment." The majority of the kids seemingly were out at the time of Charlotte's visit.

With its stench of glue and stale urine, clearly this humble abode round the back of the metro was someone's home.

A few crooked pictures hung on rusty nails hammered into the shelter walls and an old tarpaulin cover draped across two concrete pillars provided shelter from the elements.

Alejandro explained that this was not a good time to visit any of the kids because most of them had nocturnal habits and slept till well into the afternoon. Neither was it Alejandro's regular day to visit the shelter so he and Daveed had not been expected. A few of the lads did manage to rouse themselves from the security of their hidden abode and Alejandro threw a pack of cards on an overturned beer barrel, which finally drew some interest.

Charlotte was disturbed by the 'lack', sheer depravity! Yet the kids made her welcome and one young lad patted the corner of an old dusty mattress for her to sit down. He half smiled, looking suspiciously, his scrawny thin little face and empty eyes, told a story.

"*¿Hablas español?*" he asked.

"*¡Suficiente para sobrevivir!*" replied Charlotte with a gentle smile.

A cat with one eye lay nearby, with a dirty tortoiseshell coat and apricot-coloured paws, he kept his eye fixed on her. Remembering that she had a croissant smuggled out of the Hotel in case she was peckish later, she reached into her bag and pulled it out. Handing it to one of the younger boys, she watched as he pulled off a corner as though he was taking a piece of the Blessed Bread of the Holy Communion. Passing it amongst the others they each took a share. Charlotte was overwhelmed with compassion until the kid on her far right snatched what was left and wolfed it down.

"That's Mikey," said Alejandro, raising his eyebrows, not another syllable uttered, actions spoke louder than words! By the time they were due to leave, there was marginally more action in the shelter. Some interest was being shown in their new mystery visitor. Charlotte was stunned, as one older-looking *chavo* insisted on singing to her. She was astonished by the quality and excellence of his voice.

"I want to sing," he said, "want to be famous one day!" Alejandro nodded and smiled.

"His name is Hugh, short for Hugo, good isn't he?"

Charlotte was exhausted by the end of the day. Her feet were sore in spite of the fact that she had worn her most comfortable shoes! She couldn't wait to get back to her room for a hot shower, to wash away the dust and the grime and even the memories of the day's events. She needed to cry! How could she return to a cosy, if not luxurious, hotel room and think of those kids on the streets? How could she ever wash away the memories? It started to rain!

It was almost 4.30 pm before she took a taxi and returned to the hotel. Peering through the drizzle on the window, she noticed a street sign - *Calle Inocente*, where she saw a cluster of young women gathering on the corner exchanging conversation. One of them dressed all in red caught her glance, her face was badly bruised and swollen. Charlotte quickly looked away, afraid to stare.

* * *

The next day Charlotte wanted to see more. This was the very reason she had come to Mexico City, commonly known as *Distrito Federal*.

Falling accidentally upon a site while searching the Internet, she discovered the plight of the street children. Babies abandoned on the streets, not a rarity but a common occurrence! Young children not knowing what it was to have shelter, security and the satisfaction of a full belly, or the warmth of a mother's arms around them.

Charlotte being a woman of faith had called out to God and now she believed this was her destiny – her purpose for being in Mexico. With the measure of faith she had in her heart and knowing that her God would protect her, Charlotte's research had just begun. She spent two days with Alejandro and Daveed on the streets and was very impressed by their tireless energy and commitment to the kids, whose lives they were desperately trying to change. The program was not to assist the kids on the streets, but to encourage them to a life off the streets, to give them an option for life. The kids could, and did, survive on the streets, begging, stealing, some working, but for what purpose? There was no future, the Crisis Teams aimed to re-educate them, show them there was something better!

"Our success rates are quite good," said Alejandro. "It's a long slow process, the streets are in their veins."

One major factor about the Crisis Centre was that they only focused on kids from about eight years upwards, and Charlotte was keen to know what became of the abandoned babies. Having established that there were several rescue centres for the *chiquitas*, as they were called, she took a local taxi and set out to explore them. By chance, she also met Father Jose, the priest at the local church, who, when he was not preaching the Good News, was out rescuing children. Father Jose, known as Pepi to the *chavos*, was adorable, a man of God with personality and charisma, he was direct and genuine: told it as it was! It was evident why the children adored him and he was just in the process of establishing his own *Hogar de Niños*.

Later research and a chance meeting with a very lovely Mexican lady became the beginning of an amazing trail in Charlotte's life, leading to what could only be described as divine appointments, business connections and a romantic link.

CHAPTER 14
THE BABY IN
THE BASURA

It was mid-afternoon and the cooking smells
from the market traders were drifting towards
the shelter. As usual there were those who cooked
food at the roadside and in the market lanes and sold
it to those passing by.

Dolita was hungry but dare not ask the traders for
food again. She appreciated only too well that they
had been good to her but they had to earn a living,
which they would never do whilst giving the profits
to the likes of her.

"*¡Mira…!* Look!" whispered Manolo. "Over there."

Dolita looked in the direction of his gaze and there in the distance was the cutest little *conejo* she had ever seen. He scampered over towards the shelter and then hesitated pricking up his ears and twitching his nose.

Manolo was hungry too.

"Wow…!" he said. "Shall we eat him?" Catch him Dolita quick. Catch him, Rocia can cook him."

Dolita looked horrified.

"*¡Vale! ¡Vale! Es un chiste,*" he said. Let's take a walk over to the *basura* and see what we can find."

Dolita sighed a sigh of relief. She was hungry but the thought of killing the sweet little *conejo* and eating it didn't bear thinking about.

"*¡Es un chiste! ¡Un chiste!*" said Manolo again, "As if! *¡Vamos a ver!*" he chortled, "we will find something to eat." Off they went.

Angelina, who felt unwell that day, stayed behind.

They walked a while and passed spare land where a group of other kids were playing football. Someone had a radio playing loud and music filled the air, many of the songs in English: they took no notice. A little further on they came to a filthy dumping ground. Today was strangely quiet, unlike most days when the place was saturated with kids.

Dolita thought she saw Pablo Molina in the distance but didn't take too much notice as, thankfully, there was no longer any feud between them.

An old abandoned vehicle had appeared. It had not been there a few days earlier and already someone seemed to have made claim to it. Peering through the windows Dolita could see signs of life and jumped, startled by a dirty face, which emerged from a blanket pressing its nose against the window. The face was disturbing, his eyes were like two oversized black pupils, almost with a look of evil, she knew that sadly it was a deformity. Ma Kensie had told her about the kid, poor thing! Pulling the blanket over his head he disappeared once again.

Some old tyres were being used by a group of younger kids who were having fun and seemed not to have a care in the world. An old woman was on her hands and knees carefully sifting though a pile of obnoxious junk.

Dolita began to wade through the rubbish, her eyes searching for something purposeful when she suddenly heard a noise, something like a muffled cry. She ignored it at first thinking it was a figment of her imagination. "There it goes again," she said. "Listen Manolo, do you hear that?"

"Never heard nothing," said Manolo, rummaging through what appeared to be a very interesting pile of bottles and cartons.

"Listen, listen, it sounds like a baby!" exclaimed Dolita and began to frantically search through the pile of grunge to her left. Following the muffled sound and pulling herself higher into the pile of discarded rubbish she lost her footing. Slipping backwards, tumbling and hurtling, she soon hit the bottom of the mound, landing face down in a disgusting pile of rotten vegetation, hitting the side of her head on the shell of an old discarded washing machine.

For a few seconds everything went black, momentarily she thought she was going to die.

"Jesus," she managed to whisper, remembering that Old Ma Kensie had told her if ever in a frightening predicament to call on the name of Jesus. Well she did, wondering if this Jesus would suddenly appear and then aware of the pain in her head, she heard the voice of Manolo in the distance.

"Don't move," he shouted as he clambered over to rescue her. Dolita lay dazed for a few moments, Manolo looking alarmingly into her eyes, he too wondering if she was going to die.

Dolita's vision was momentarily blurred. Thinking she was seeing double she soon realised Pablo Molina was standing beside Manolo. "Where did he come from?" Dolita said frostily looking at Manolo. He didn't answer.

"Well don't just stare, pull me up," she whimpered, bravely trying to disregard the seething pain and the feeling of something wet and sticky, running down the side of her head. She feared it was blood but remembering the very thing that had caused her to fall in the first place she was more concerned about the strange noises than her own well-being.

A sigh of relief. "Oh you scared me!" exclaimed Manolo.

"I'm OK, just fine, don't fuss."

"Take my hand," said Pablo softly, his voice fading to a whisper, reaching out towards her and smiling. Dolita was soon back on her feet! Manolo was not impressed; he flinched. In fact, he was quite irritated by Pablo's presence. Dolita was his mate and Pablo should mind his own flipping business. Snarling at Pablo who had helped Dolita to her feet, Pablo quickly sensed Manolo's indignation and he was gone as quick as he had appeared.

"Well, where did he come from?" she asked Manolo curiously. Before getting an answer, the muffled cry that she had heard earlier echoed deep into her very being. Suddenly the pain from her head was hardly noticeable as she focused on the task in hand. To rescue what she believed was a baby.

Manolo admired her guts and determination, that quality, making her different from the other kids, he helped her up the banking of dross and rubbish, trying to check her head at the same time for cuts and signs of bleeding.

"Oh my! Ergh! Dolita you're bleeding all over, keep still will you?" he said, steadying her as she was clearly showing signs of dizziness and disorientation after her fall.

"Sort me out later," she remonstrated, tossing things aside frantically, "it's about 'ere," she called, looking towards some old milk cartons and rotting cabbages. The stench was vile: rats and birds all competing for the leftovers. Manolo pinched his nose and grimaced as Dolita carried on searching.

She finally uncovered a box, little bigger than a shoe box. It had been chewed in the corner by rats but for the most part it was intact. Carefully lifting it and placing it gently beside her, she precariously removed the lid, a thin lemon blanket concealed the contents. Unwrapping it, she gasped.

"¡Mira! Chiquita, chiquita. It's a baby, oh look what I've found." "It's a baby." "It's a baby!" she cried out in anguish.

"A baby what?" came the voice of another kid who had scrambled over to see what perpetrated such a commotion.

He swore. "It's a baby. A real baby!" he exclaimed. Manolo said nothing, his mouth fell wide open in amazement: perfectly positioned for catching flies, of which there were plenty hovering around the dump!

Dolita had heard rumours of babies being dumped in the *basura*, but seeing with her own eyes she could not believe.

She remembered how her own mother had left her in the streets, but she was much older and she had left her in the care of Old Ma Kensie after all. But this, oh my gosh, why would anyone do such an awful thing. To leave a baby in the *basura*! To be so cruel and heartless? Dolita thought her heart was breaking.

"Whoever… whoever could do such a thing to a little chiquita?" she cried out, tears in her eyes, her heart hurting now far more than her head.

"Be quick!" bellowed Manolo, disturbed by the appearance of the buzzards overhead. Their wingspan was enormous and he knew they were looking for small mammals to devour.

"What shall we do?" he yelled, looking at the baby. "It's so tiny and wrinkly. I think it's only a few days old."

"Well we can't look after it that's for sure," said Dolita looking at the baby who stared straight back at her in bewilderment." Better find Ma Kensie, she will know what to do."

Picking up the box gently, frightened to take the tiny little bundle out in case she hurt it, Dolita and Manolo set off to find the old beggar woman.

Walking slowly, but wanting to run, her heart pounding she carried the box most carefully. Manolo was walking thoughtfully by her side. The cries she had heard earlier had now ceased and the babe did not make a muff.

Where was Ma Kensie when you needed her? Typical where was she?

It seemed like hours before they found the old woman, in reality it was probably only ten or fifteen minutes.

Ma Kensie knew exactly what to do. She immediately summoned Martinez who was standing next to his taxi, the old, battered green and white Beetle at the other side of the *calle*.

How odd, how very very odd! Martinez was talking to none other than Pablo Molina. How come he was suddenly popping up all over. A few minutes ago he had come to her rescue at the *basura* and why was he here talking to Martinez? This was not even his patch of town. Well she hadn't time to reason it out and thankfully, this was one occasion when Martinez's taxi was not out of action, parked up in Dodgy Deuno's garage.

Martinez, obviously greatly alarmed when he realised the

situation, agreed to take the baby to the *Oficina de la Procuraduría* at the other side of town, but he insisted that he did not go alone and Dolita would have to go with him to explain the mysterious find! She wouldn't have done any other. Frankly someone had to care for the baby while he drove! Ushering her into the back of the cab quickly, they were off leaving Pablo and Manolo in a whirlwind. The offices of the Procuraduría were at least 20 minutes drive and the traffic as usual was heavy.

If only they had taken the baby to the local *policía* she thought but Ma Kensie had clearly told them where to go so Dolita assumed she knew best.

Martinez found the building having negotiated several traffic jams and escaped the congested lanes into the back streets. He was a taxi driver after all: taxi drivers knew most places and he certainly did. He swivelled and swerved until his car pulled up in front of the *Oficina de la Procuraduría*.

The building was hidden behind large, well guarded walls. Security was stringent as this was where all young rescued children were taken whether abandoned, neglected or abused. This was the initial point of rescue for the children. Those at least who did get rescued.

By now the baby which Dolita had taken from the box and held so preciously was beginning to look like a lifeless doll. Not a sound came from its frail, listless body, its eyes now closed but earlier they had looked at her pale and sunken, helpless and afraid. Dolita shuddered and began to wonder if it were still alive.

She had not bothered to discern whether it were a boy or a girl. A shudder went from the top of her head to the tip of her toes as she thought of the possibility of nursing a dead baby.

Her face grimaced and her knuckles turned white. The palms of her hands were sweaty as she held onto the lifeless bundle.

Martinez abandoned the taxi in a restricted area outside the *Procuraduría*. Praying that it would not be noticed, afraid that it might be towed away, but as a matter of urgency he had no option. He rushed round to open the door for the young Dolita. She was now looking decidedly pale and traumatised herself. Not only had she suffered that awful fall and a blow to the head but also she had undergone the horrific shock of discovering the chiquita. A trauma for anyone let alone someone who was barely nine.

Adding to her anxiety was the fact that she too was an abandoned kid, and the Procuraduría may see it appropriate to keep her as well.

The time was not right to start sorting out her own life although the words "no kids should live on the streets" were going round and round in her head: her pretty little head, which by now was pounding and feeling as though a sharp instrument was being forced into her temple. Dolita had never had a headache like this before. She felt stiffening in her lower neck and her body was beginning to feel bruised and sore. Her left thigh particularly hurt where she had banged it. Concealing her anxieties in her concern for the baby her mind drifted.

The streets for all their misery and worth were still her home. The street kids, the market traders, Old Ma Kensie and Martinez were her family. Even the thought of not seeing Dodgy Deuno again she could not bear.

Being ushered into the cool, spacious reception as if in a whirlwind, Dolita felt the very centre of all that was happening around her and yet it was as if she were not there at all. As though she were an outsider looking in. She heard the voice of Martinez as though muffled saying, "My daughter found a baby in the *basura*," and the squeeze of Martinez's hand in hers reassured her that everything would be all right.

CHAPTER 15
LA OFICINA DE LA
PROCURADURÍA

The baby having been quickly taken from her, Dolita, sat and waited for news, while Martinez went to move his car to a safer place. She sat quietly not saying a word. Just watching and waiting, watching and waiting!

The man sitting beside her was terribly irritating. He was a big chap, broad shoulders and huge belly. The woman beside him was petite, blonde hair, dark at the roots, as Dolita would say 'painted hair' and clearly quite a timid personality. Dolita wished he would shut his mouth. She wished she could shut it for him. An aggressive train of thought for someone normally as sweet and mild-mannered as the young Dolita, but his voice droned continuously: a critical personality, he grumbled incessantly.

He was brazen, angry and Dolita questioned how two people so different came to be a couple or an item, as clearly they were.

His body language revealed all. Keeping his arms folded, rested on his big fat belly, leaning back in his chair, he behaved as though he owned the *Distrito Federal*. He certainly had a very high opinion of himself.

"The obnoxious beast…!" she muttered under her breath. What could possibly be their reason for being in the *Oficina de la Procuraduría*? She felt sure it was not for the purpose of doing anyone a kind deed.

Dolita sat mortified to hear him bragging about the watch he had just bought. "30,000 dollars and cheap at the price," he exclaimed to the woman sitting beside him.

Dolita felt sickened! Where was the justice in the world? Children sniffing glue to take away the hunger pains, babies in the *basura* abandoned by a desperate mum, no doubt something that she would one day live to regret. In comparison, the man sitting next to her, an over-fed, obtrusive, ignorant, aggressive character, clearly with more money than sense. Maybe he was at the Procuraduría to make a big, fat donation to the excellent rescue work they did there. "Uhm. Better not judge," she thought.

The noticeable point being, for all his money, he was still not happy with his life, the grumpy, miserable old soul.

"True riches did not come from material things Old Ma Kensie would say. Whoever loves money never has enough. Whoever loves wealth is never satisfied with his income."

Dolita, deep in thought - many a wise word came from Old Ma Kensie's lips, did not notice as the door opened and Martinez peered round cautiously, entering the room. He moved towards her, stumbling over the petite woman's handbag, which she had left clumsily near the door.

"Oops, sorry," she muttered nervously, moving it aside.

"Stupid woman!" came the brazen voice of her partner.

"I bet he gives her a hard time," whispered Dolita to Martinez as he sat beside her, raising his bushy eyebrows.

Today was a day surely she would never forget for as long as she lived.

Amazingly, she had managed to disguise her fall from Martinez. He had been too concerned with getting rid of the baby and I say that in the nicest possible sense.

Martinez being very worried about the chiquita and anxious to secure its safety, had not noticed the trickle of dried blood on the side of Dolita's head. He had jumped into his cab and concentrated on the drive to the Procuraduría. As usual, at this time the traffic was horrendous. As Dolita sat in the back of the Volkswagen Martinez had been oblivious to her injury, her thick raggy hair concealed the evidence of the blow.

Ten minutes passed, half an hour passed, one hour and they were still waiting for news of the baby. Martinez finally made his report as best he could. Dolita chipping in with comments of one or two syllables in agreement. A young woman, probably a nurse, in a plain white crisp dress and flat soft tennis shoes, offered Dolita a drink of ice-cold water, for which she felt eternally grateful.

No points for observation, she too failed to notice the little girl's injury, and thought she was just tired and stressed.

By now the beads of sweat were beginning to run down Dolita's back, she felt quite nauseous, and Martinez knew that he had to get her out of there, somewhere quiet where she could rest. He assumed her worsening condition was due to sheer exhaustion, not to mention the trauma of the whole event. At the first opportune moment they left discreetly, in the knowledge that the baby was in capable hands, had been seen by a *médico* and would be OK. Just OK!

"Whew," a sigh of relief from Dolita and Martinez, simultaneously. She really wanted to jump for joy but couldn't muster the energy to hop on one foot, let alone jump. Martinez had given his address and as much information as he could knowing that a social worker would be in contact later.

* * *

"Please sign the visitors' book, Señorita," said the receptionist as two, well-dressed women stood waiting to see the *Directora*.

Martinez took little notice of them but Dolita caught the woman's heel and mumbled an apology as they turned to leave the building.

"*¡No problema!*" she said, smiling and before another moment passed they were ushered into the *Directora*'s waiting room and Martinez whisked Dolita away.

The traffic was now worse than ever and Martinez was anxious to get Dolita back to the shelter. It took him nearly 90 minutes to go a short distance.

Unbelievable!! Absolutely unbelievable!!

He was sure that after a long sleep, she would be just fine. It was not practical to take her to his own home which was already grossly overcrowded with his own wife, two children, a new baby, plus his brother's family who were also staying with them: they had been turned out of their own house for non-payment of rent, the previous week.

Well she would be fine at the shelter, he was sure of that. Rocia the motherly one of the group would take care of her.

The fact was Martinez left Dolita at the shelter expecting Rocia to turn up shortly afterwards. As it happened she had gone away for a few days. Manolo, Angelina and some of the other boys were the only ones at the shelter, even Enrique and Hugh the older boys were not around. Manolo who had been with Dolita at the dump knew about the dreadful fall, but before he was able to say anything to Martinez, he was gone. For some strange reason neither Enrique nor Hugh returned that day, and Manolo and Angelina tucked Dolita up in the corner of the shelter. They covered her with a pile of blankets, dirty but warm! They hoped that Martinez was right, and that after a long sleep she would be just fine, unfortunately that was not the case.

* * *

The two women sat in the *Directora*'s office; an assistant offered them a cool glass of water. Charlotte listened intently fighting back the tears, as the *Directora* told her how many babies had been abandoned on the streets, doorsteps, in churches, gardens and the *basura*.

"It's actually a federal offence to abandon a baby and the ultimate punishment could be imprisonment. Unfortunately, it still happens and a recent report, published this year, shows that 81 babies have been abandoned in the last fifteen months," the *Directora* said.

"Tragic, what on earth possesses a mother to do such a thing?" asked Charlotte.

"Oh..! A number of reasons!" replied the *Directora*. "Desperation usually, psychological problems, extreme family pressures, sickness and addictions. Let me explain… three babies were found in the *basura* recently and have been very poorly; one needed emergency surgery, rats…!"

Charlotte didn't answer, she wanted to vomit.

"Sorry," said the *Directora*, "but that is the severity of the problem that we have here. There are people in *Distrito Federal* doing a wonderful job but it's not enough." And the *Directora* gave up her lunch break to spend time with Charlotte, explaining the predicament of the street kids, and the plight of the abandoned babies.

"Shall we go for a late lunch?" Asked Claudia Graciela, the Mexican lady who had escorted Charlotte to the *Oficina de la Procuraduría* and had become both her confidante and friend. "Don't feel much like eating," she replied. "I know, but you have not eaten all day and you'll be no good to anyone if you don't take care of yourself." She looked at Charlotte's face which was crumpled with sadness.

"Come on," said Claudia Graciela, "we are going to eat. I know just the place and then I'm going to show you some of the wonderful babies that have been rescued: one in particular who is going to adoptive parents in the States next month. There are some happy endings," she said. "Here in Mexico it's not all doom and gloom" and smiling, she ushered Charlotte towards the parked car.

"Blast, the traffic is heavy!"

"Rush hour?" enquired Charlotte.

"No such thing in Mexico D.F. it's always like this! And it's Friday, day pay."

"Pay day," said Charlotte, correcting her and managing a smile.

Angelina became concerned about Dolita's worsening condition and she was so worried she went in search of Rosa the cheese lady, early the next morning. Angelina was barely recovered from her own sickness having had vile stomach cramps the previous day. Otherwise she would have undoubtedly gone to the dump and been there when they had discovered the baby.

Dolita groaned. She looked ill. Her little body was hot, very hot. She was sweating profusely, yet she shivered so much that her teeth began to chatter. Dolita now complained that she could hardly move, her body stiffening and aching with pain which seemed to be everywhere, the poor little girl looked frightened. Today of all days, Rosa had not turned up. Weird, very weird thought Angelina. She looked alarmingly at the space where she usually placed her rickety stall. Feeling very anxious she sped back to the shelter, colliding with Alejandro as she hurtled round the corner.

"Am I glad to see you!" she screeched as she began to blurt out an explanation of Dolita's condition, ushering Alejandro over to her huddled friend in the corner.

Alejandro's appearance was a miracle indeed. It was Friday, he never visited on Fridays.

"She has a high temperature," said Alejandro.

"Uhm… she keeps mumbling about strange stuff and bright lights, think she's gone *loca* or something."

"Maybe 'cos she bumped her head," said Manolo telling them about the fall at the *basura* the previous day and the amazing discovery.

"No wonder you feel so bad!" exclaimed Alejandro. "I expect in a few days you will have some real bruises. Sounds like you were lucky, you could have broken a leg or something. Let's take a look at your head."

Seeing the gash in her head, well camouflaged by her matted thick hair, he exclaimed, "I don't believe it! This kid sure has guts, poor little mite, she's taken a nasty blow to the head, that's for sure, and overcome all in her determination to see that little chiquita safe! We'll have to get someone to take a look at you young lady, and now, right now!"

Dolita whined, she sounded pitiful.

"Leave this to me," said Alejandro and a few phone calls later Dolita found herself on the way to the city hospital, Alejandro by her side.

CHAPTER 16
A BATH AND A DOLL

When Dolita was admitted to the hospital, Alejandro took care of the formalities, hanging around for a couple of hours until she was settled. One of the first tasks was to be seen by the *médico* and check her head injury. The wound had long since stopped bleeding but needed cleaning, thankfully not stitching. Three cuts were cleaned and then glued much to Dolita's amusement.

Her head was hurting and she thought it quite hilarious that it was to be glued. She had never imagined such a thing. Wait till she told the others! Dolita's head injury however, soon turned out to be only part of the problem. She fell asleep, exhausted and feverish.

"This kid smells," said the skinny, sullen-faced duty nurse pinching her nose and wrinkling her face.

"So would you smell if you lived on the streets," snapped her colleague angrily. Consequently, the nurse with more empathy, the cheerful round face and compassionate eyes, called Marta, took care of Dolita thereafter.

For several days she nursed her, bathed her and washed her hair. She gave her medicine which of course Dolita hated, thinking it tasted more like poison, "cat's pee" or something, not that she had ever tasted cat's pee!

The first bath time was quite an event! The bathroom smelt clinical, but pleasant. The way Dolita imagined a beauty parlour, potions and powders, lotions and creams. She lay in the hot tub immersed in bubbles - the first time in her life: a mixture between a wonderful feeling and a harrowing experience. What if she fell asleep and drowned? Relieved that Marta didn't leave her alone, she relished in the pleasurable feelings, until Marta took a peculiar looking comb to her hair and tugged. She screamed: it hurt! Applying a slimy pink potion and leaving for a while, Marta showed her the lice as she combed them away. Barely seen by the naked eye, they were just visible.

"The comb breaks their legs," Marta said, "stops 'em breeding! We'll have to do this again tomorrow," she tutted, being careful not to wet the area that had been glued.

Dolita enjoyed the pampering until Marta signaled her to get out, passing her a huge fluffy white towel, large enough to wrap around her little body at least three times.

She felt deliciously clean and Marta offered her a pale-lemon nightgown to slip into and clipped her hair out of her eyes, with tiny, delicate clips, allowing it to dry naturally after squeezing out the excess water. The hair clips were elegant; too pretty an adornment for Dolita, not her thing! However, Angelina would have loved them.

She planned to keep them and smuggle them out for her special friend. Meanwhile the kindly nurse listened to her stories of life on the streets.

"It sounds awful," said the nurse. "How do you survive?"

"Just do. I get by with a little help from my friends," giggled Dolita. No choice really, we have to survive. I'm one of the lucky ones, me and the other kids in the shelter, well we stick together. The Street Kid Code you know."

"Oooh," said the nurse, intrigued. "What's that?"

"Well I suppose you would say it's the rules. Survival and all that."

"Tell me more."

"It's easy to say, not so easy to do.

Rule 1: If you have it, share it!

Rule 2: If a kid's in trouble, be there!

Rule 3: If a kid wants to talk, listen.

Rule 4: If you make a promise, keep it.

Rule 5: If he confides in you, don't betray him."

She hesitated on rule 6.

"Rule 6: Never mock, ridicule or be cruel to a street kid."

Oops! She really must stop calling people a *necio*! she thought.

"Rule 7: Treat other kids the way you would like them to treat you.

Rule 8: Respect one another, treating everyone as equal.

No lesser.

Survival's the game.

Rule number one is the hardest of all to keep."

"Uhm… I quite understand. I suppose it's hard to share when you don't have much in the first place."

"Too true," said Dolita. "You try sharing your only bread roll with half a dozen other kids when you have not eaten for days."

"It doesn't bear thinking about," said Marta, looking alarmed, fortunately she had never been in such a situation. "I suppose we take every thing for granted."

"Most of the kids in our shelter are quite good, even Mikey Mean is not so mean as he used to be. Once though, before the saga of the stolen bike, he was dreadful. He would not share anything."

Dolita recited the tale of when he came back from the market with several avocados, "He greedily ate one and stashed the others under his part of the mattress.

"He was saving them for later and no one else was going to get hold of one, that was for sure. Some of the younger boys watched hopefully but dare not say anything to him, they were afraid of igniting his angry temper. In those days Mikey was not well liked as you can imagine.

"The sad thing was most of the avocados were wasted 'cos they went off. You see Mikey forgot about them. So did the other kids too. A few days later Mikey put his hand under the mattress, they were all rotten and infested."

"Oh how vile," said Marta. Dolita giggled.

"So what changed Mikey?" asked Marta.

"The kids all rallied round to help him when the Molina brothers put a wanted sign on his head. Those Molina brothers really scared him. He thought he was tough until he came up against little Pablo Molina's elder brothers. It took lots of grovelling

146

I'll tell you to get them off his back. Enrique and Hugh sorted it out, and me too," she said proudly. "Finally peace was restored and Mikey has been better since then. He realises we need one another now more than ever, know what I mean?"

Marta, nodded her head. She thought she did.

"So not everyone sticks to the code then?" asked Marta.

"No of course not, and there are rival gangs, like the Molinas, but the thing about any gang, they usually look out for their own. For the most part, the kids in our shelter do, too."

"Speaking of friends, someone came to visit you earlier when you were sleeping. Slipped in and out before I had chance to get his name."

"Oh?" puzzled Dolita thinking it must be Manolo or one of the others, but surprised that they had been anywhere near the hospital, let alone been allowed in. How on earth would a scruffy street kid get into the building without being seen, she pondered.

"What did he look like?" she asked.

"Oh rather tough-looking, he puffed his chest out proudly when he caught sight of me, grinned and disappeared quickly. Come to think of it he had a really cheeky expression, bet he's a real character. Rather flamboyant he was too, you could see him a mile away in that flash red waistcoat."

Dolita puzzled all the more, that was certainly not Manolo, he would not be seen dead in red, he absolutely hated the colour; despised it!

Well, perhaps it was not someone looking for her after all, maybe it was the wrong bed!

Marta took a great interest in the young Dolita and her concerns were very real for the little girl.

"We will have to find somewhere for her to live, she cannot go back to the streets."

Dolita could hear the voices discussing her future, as though she were not even there. It was Marta talking to Alejandro who had been to visit her and was just about to leave.

"I wish it was so simple," said Alejandro. "The streets are all that she knows. For all the misery and strife they are her home. Before we can take a child off the streets we have to take the streets out of the child. It has to be done gradually over a period of time. To take a kid like Dolita and suddenly institutionalise her, she just simply couldn't handle it," he explained. "She would just run away."

Marta was not convinced and intended to make her own enquiries.

Dolita began to thrive in the hospital and all the staff became very fond of her. Moreover, by the time she was due to leave, they all adored her. Such a brave girl, an act of great courage, the rumour was she'd saved the life of a baby. She became the life and soul of the ward and was renowned for her mischievous, infamous giggle.

As she began to regain her strength, she certainly enjoyed the warm comfortable bed and the abundance of food. Forgetting about her mysterious visitor, she was now missing her family, the street kids, the shelter. Yes in spite of everything it was home and she wanted to go home. More importantly, what of Raggy Man? How she missed her adorable Raggy Man.

Hearing the voices of the Crisis Team in the adjacent office, this time, Alejandro, Daveed and other workers were discussing her. "Here we go again!" thought Dolita as she listened to the conversation, her bed conveniently situated close to the thin partitioning office wall.

"She's too young to live on the streets," they said, "but what can we do? Where can she go?"

"Do you know how many kids live on the streets?" interrupted Dolita, peering round the office door. "Have you really any idea?

"Don't talk about me, talk to me," she snapped angrily as Alejandro turned towards her.

"Sometimes I hate it, but it's all I know, the streets are my home."

"Told you so," said Alejandro

Dolita thought of Mikey Mean, Roberto and the twins. If she left the streets then they would have to come too! Yes, they would all have to come, and so the discussion went on.

The next day Dolita looked around her dormitory; ten beds in all, hers at the end. All of the kids had stuff, heaps of stuff, brought in by mothers and other concerned relatives who visited them daily. The girls seemed to have dolls, cuddly stuff, bears and things. She was determined one day to see her mother and one day she too would have a doll, a *muñeca* to call her own! Unlike any other, yes a special *muñeca*!

Yes, she would have a very special *muñeca*!

Later that evening Dolita lay subdued in her bed. The other kids didn't dare visit her in the hospital and they certainly would not let them in if they tried. Oh, Rosa managed to call one day so she did feel a little "loved up" then, at least. She had completely forgotten about the mystery visitor assuming he wasn't for her.

Trying to dismiss the pain of not having a mother to visit her like the others, all at once she saw her! It was as though she took over her thought pattern and there she was. Suspended in mid-air, about two feet away. Dolita wanted to reach out but dare not. Real or imaginary she knew not. She understood not, but she could see her, every tiny detail.

She was truly beautiful. Like a rag doll, the most beautiful doll she had ever seen. Her legs were long and slender. Her body slim, she had a pretty round face, with freckles around and above her nose.

Her clothes were vibrant, the colours captivating. She wore a plain bright red t-shirt and striped dungarees. The diagonal stripes looked as though all the colours of the rainbow had been taken and carefully sewn into them forming each vibrant stripe. Red and yellow and pink and green, orange and violet and blue. The colours were so passionate, so  strong. On her feet she wore black satin boots with pretty laces and on her head a baseball cap, plain but inscribed with the initial "R" in the centre of the peak. Her hair was long, exceptionally long and perfectly plaited in two pigtails which fell below her waist. A thin strip of scarlet red ribbon was tied at the end of each plait. Finally she had a petite, scarlet purse with a long thin shoulder strap which she wore over her right shoulder and which rested on her left hip. She was so lovely, so appealing.

Dolita soaked in the vision enjoying every second and then suddenly she was gone... disturbed abruptly by the voice of Marta, bringing her favourite chocolate drink.

"What is it, what are you looking at?" questioned Marta. Dolita's gaze transferred and as quickly as she had appeared, she was gone.

"Oh, just dreaming!" replied Dolita trying to reason in her mind the strange happening she had just experienced.

How could it be a dream, she was not asleep? So was it her imagination or some sort of vision? Old Ma Kensie once talked about visions. A supernatural or prophetic apparition she would say. Well whatever, it certainly was a mystery. Dolita decided not to share her mystery with Marta but to hide it in her heart; she gratefully accepted the chocolate drink and settled down to go to sleep! Life is so full of mysteries she thought!

On reflection, I don't think anyone completely realised how much the brave little girl had suffered the day she found the baby in the *basura*. The truth was she had been very ill. The blow to the head had left Dolita slightly concussed and an X-ray later showed severe bruising and some slight internal bleeding. With bed rest she would recover. There was fear at first that she might have to wear a brace or a collar to diffuse any possible damage done to the neck and spinal column. Fortunately, that did not become necessary, but eating was certainly a problem for a couple of weeks. The facial muscles, particularly those of the jaw were very bruised and sore. She ate, drank and even spoke with great difficulty. An added problem was that Dolita had a touch of leishmaniasis, a viral disease similar to malaria. It was usually carried by an insect or midges and in this instance had been brought about by a sandfly bite on the upper thigh. The poison had gone into her little body causing a severe viral infection. It was more than likely that she was bitten while rummaging through the rubbish at the dump.

It actually took several weeks to regain her strength fully. The infection had left her feeling weak and as Dolita said, as weak as a newborn kitten, having heard the expression from one of the nurses in the hospital. She did wonder however, how they knew what a newborn kitten felt like?

CHAPTER 17
RETURNING HOME

Nearly three weeks passed and Dolita returned to the shelter in spite of efforts to get her into an *Hogar de Niños*. She did agree to spend more time with Alejandro and stay at least two nights a week at the Crisis Centre, but in actual fact that never happened.

Marta was very distraught to see her go but did not have the means to change the situation.

Settling back into street life, dark days followed.

Angelina tried desperately to cheer her and even offered to lend her Pygmy for a few days!

Pygmy, by the way, was now a strong little character, quite aware that Angelina was instrumental in saving his life, he was happy to potter around the undergrowth near the shelter. Having moved from the handbag to a comfortable little den, he had made it cosy, full of leaves and moss, he thought it was the most perfect of little abodes.

Pygmy did find his way back into the precious purple satin bag when Angelina decided they were going out, but he couldn't do much about that! Angelina was bigger than him!

It was when the sky had been like a blanket of grey for a few days that Dolita felt an overwhelming emptiness and depression engulfing her.

She was very disturbed because since her admission to hospital, Raggy Man had simply disappeared. Had he fretted in her absence? Either way she was desperate to find him.

Dolita felt like crying, but certainly wasn't going to, street kids didn't cry! She had to be tough! How else could she survive?

Choking back the tears, suddenly she could bear it no longer, her eyes full, they began to pour. If she could have collected those tears she would have filled a bottle, one bottle, two bottles, maybe more. The sadness overwhelmed her.

Blast, now she felt like a weakling. Wiping away the salty wetness from her face, she couldn't bear the thought of anyone realising she had cried. For sure, taking a deep breath and with an enormous sigh, she was not going to be so weak ever again!

Where was Raggy Man?

She missed him so much. Not that Raggy Man was much help when it came to conversation but at least he seemed to understand her. He would sit beside her, his little head tilted to the side, his ears erect as if listening to her every word, gazing at her quizzingly as she poured out her heart's desires. If only he could talk, he knew all the secrets of the streets. Raggy Man, oh where was her precious Raggy man?

As sweet as Angelina's intentions were, and as comical as Pygmy could be, he was hardly a substitute for Raggy.

It was the rainy season and Dolita was so desperately fed up with the cold, damp, shelter nights. She began to daydream. She thought of her mother and how she imagined her to be. She remembered her time in the hospital. The warm cosy bed, deliciously clean sheets and fluffy soft white pillows. She remembered the abundance of food and the scrumptious chocolate drink that Marta gave her every night before she settled down to sleep. Known as ColaCoa, she preferred to drink it hot, while others chose it cold.

She reflected on the pleasure as the hot water spilled over her frail little body as she took a shower and how Marta had scolded her for staying in too long and wasting water. The shower as it pulsated and massaged her limbs was breathtaking.

Some of the girls had dolls. How she wished she too had a doll. Something to hold, something to call her own. Something she did not have to share.

Suddenly the sound of a car backfiring in the distance brought her back to reality. In your dreams! Indeed she thought. How ridiculous. She was a street kid. Tough at that. A survivor! Who ever heard of a street kid wanting a doll, and at her age too. Surely she was now too old for a doll anyway.

Pull yourself together she thought wiping her eyes and her nose on the same sleeve and she set off to find Raggy Man.

Fortunately, later that day Raggy did turn up and Dolita was furious with him.

"Don't you ever frighten me like that again!" she cried, scooping him up and tucking him under her left arm, with such a sigh of relief, she squeezed him tight. Raggy thought he was going to choke and gasped for air. Although he loved Dolita like no other, he was glad when she released her grip.

"Come on Raggy, now I have you back there is something we must do," she said, thinking of the next task in hand. "I don't care how long it takes, but somehow we are going to find my mum! Let's start with Old Ma Kensie".

Raggy Man yapped, once again pleased to be reunited with his very special friend and off they went together to find the old beggar woman. She never did find out where he had been. "Poor Raggy," she thought, "he had probably missed her as much as she had missed him." Indeed, Raggy had, and he was determined to stay close to her from now on.

They finally found Ma Kensie in a most peculiar position, bottom in the air, head in the drain.

"What on earth are you doing Ma Kensie?" enquired Dolita.

Ma Kensie turned her head and smiled a gummy smile: the startled kid reeled backwards in horror.

"Oh, Ma Kensie!" she cried. "Where are your teeth?"

"Lost em, they fell out, down 'ere somewhere, got to find 'em."

"What, all of them? Oh yuk, do you really want them back if they have been in the sewer?"

"No choice," she said, "need me teeth, no money to get any more."

The helpless Dolita looked on in a quandary as Ma Kensie continued her search.

"How can they just fall out?" asked Dolita looking very puzzled and at the same time, now very concerned about the old woman's plight.

"Did so! she said, they weren't me teeth anyway."

"Whaaaat…!" exclaimed Dolita, "whooose… were they?"

She had never heard of such a thing! It didn't bear thinking about.

Ma Kensie muttered something as she continued her search. Twenty years ago having had the teeth made for her, something about her gums shrinking, and now the teeth did not fit so well.

Dolita had never heard of anyone having teeth made for them but thought now was not the time for questions and better help the poor old woman search. What a horrible dilemma, but as usual Raggy Man came to the rescue.

After searching wholeheartedly for ages, Raggy Man barked and produced the teeth. A grateful and most delighted Ma Kensie rinsed them in a nearby barrel of rain water, and put them in her mouth, shifting them around until they settled into the right position.

Dolita felt sick "but needs must", she thought. She had lots of respect for the old beggar woman, and often looked to her for instruction and guidance. Although she didn't actually know much about her background she seemed to have lots of wisdom, and a wealth of knowledge.

Something which comes with age I suppose, but it would be interesting one day to hear Old Ma Kensie's story and how she came to live on the streets.

For now the question was to find out about Dolita's family and this she intended to do.

"Tell me about my mother," asked Dolita looking with earnest into Old Ma Kensie's weathered face and muddy brown eyes. "Tell me about my family! What do you know about them?"

"Why do you want to know?" asked Ma Kensie. She reflected for a moment, "It's past, it's gone, you live 'ere now." She grinned and shook her head backwards and forwards, to the left and the right, checking the teeth were well seated.

"Just do," replied Dolita, "just want to know."

Her little face was taught with pain as she thought of her mother and how she imagined her to be. Just like the young woman in the charcoal sketch. Yes, the one that she had found in the old wooden box at the house, *Casa Ana Maria 247*. Dolita liked her. She would do just fine as a mother. Dolita never did show the box or the picture to Ma Kensie. Come to think of it she never did tell Ma Kensie about the discovery of the house at 247.

"Well," said Ma Kensie, pulling her scruffy black shawl over her shoulders and fastening the only button that was left hanging by a single thread on her tatty red cardigan.

"I must try and find her a new cardigan," thought Dolita. "Yes, next time I go to the dump I will see what I can find. One person's rubbish was another person's best, and she decided that she would search every *basura* until she found her very old friend a cardigan. Dolita snuggled down beside the old woman pulling the plastic sheet and dirty rug over them to keep out the chill of the night air. Raggy snuggled down too. They were all happy to be together.

Ma Kensie began: "You're mother came from Oaxaca: Dolita's eyes widened as she listened. Ma Kensie paused, studied and continued.

158

"The valley of Oaxaca was and still is very beautiful with a magical quality, full of hidden places and mystery. Royal palms, reaching 60 feet into the clear blue sky. Limes, lemons and pomegranates growing in their abundance. An array of wild flowers splendid in colour, coming and going with the seasons. Clumps of pale-yellow, orange, red and powder blue flowers. Birds in their plenty, chickadees, cockatiels, parakeets.

Water in the valley was a precious commodity and not to be wasted. "A place of true beauty," described Ma Kensie. "Ownership of land was established by occupation and agreement with several neighbours. Many families had come to own their small holdings and today in many parts it is little changed since its earlier inhabitants."

"Wow! You seem to know quite a lot about Oaxaca," whispered Dolita, shifting the plastic sheet and threadbare rug into a different position. Ma Kensie nodded in agreement and carried on, squinting as the sun momentarily burst from behind the clouds and vanished again.

"A typical home was a two-room shack with strips of material hanging as dividers to give a degree of privacy. Pieces of tin and rough timbers formed the parts of a lean-to and a communal toilet and shower in the courtyard was shared with adjacent properties."

By now Dolita had realised Ma Kensie could not possess so much information, particularly in such detail, unless she had been there. But something else startled the young Dolita more than her knowledge; Ma Kensie was describing Oaxaca in a way she had never heard the old women speak before. Not in her usual tongue but like a sophisticated, well-educated women. How strange, suddenly Ma Kensie was not like the old beggar woman she had always known. Puzzled, but anxious to know more, "Ma Kensie," she inquired interrupting. "Have you been to Oaxaca?"

Ma Kensie paused, sighed and said, "Yes Dolita, I have been to Oaxaca."

"Wow, Ma Kensie. Why didn't you tell me before?"

"Because I didn't and I had my reasons, so don't ask too many questions, OK!" Dolita was puzzled.

"Did you stay there for long? Did you know my mother? Did you know my family?"

"What did I just say to you?" she replied. "I will tell you this. I lived in Oaxaca for a while. I never met your great grandmother although I did have the privilege once of meeting your great grandfather."

"Ma Kensie!" howled Dolita "Why didn't you tell me this stuff before?"

"Err…. Uhmm… you never asked before…"

She hesitated, stuttered and continued, "He was a very strong and proud man, a descendant of the Mixtecs. Many times removed his great-great grandfather was a mighty warrior."

Dolita looked curiously, an expression of absolute amazement painted on her face.

"That would be your great-great-great-great grandfather or something. Your mother was just a child then. Taiawah was her name."

There was an uncomfortable silence. Dolita's heart skipped a beat. Her eyes jolted open; was this real?

160

All this time and Ma Kensie had known stuff about her family and never told her, she could hardly believe her own ears. She felt the sting of a tear and blinked quickly. Ma Kensie continued.

"When your mother Taiawah came to the city our paths crossed. Only once did I see her, the day she left you here with me and never returned. I recognised her even though she had grown from a mere child into a young woman. Something troubled her that day; in fact she was deeply troubled. She asked me if I would take care of you for a short while but she never came back." No one was more surprised than me when she didn't return."

Dolita sat quietly wondering what to make of the whole affair. Then Ma Kensie knew what her mum looked like. She could tell her more, even describe her. Was she tall, was she short. Fat or slim. Pretty or…? Of course she was pretty, she was beautiful, she was her mum and what about Ma Kensie? She, too, had a past, a secret past. Who was she really and why was she now on the streets? What was her history? How come she had met her grandfather?

Dolita was just about to open her mouth to ask…

"No more questions tonight," exclaimed Ma Kensie. "We will talk later."

"But…"

"No Dolita, later."

Dolita was frustrated but she knew "no" meant "no".

Old Ma Kensie had a saying. "Let your yes be yes and your no be no". Clearly she was not going to get anything else out of the old woman just yet.

Wanting to stamp her feet or kick someone Dolita backed off. She would wait, but didn't intend to wait long. This was serious stuff and if Ma Kensie knew something, she would prise it out of her later.

The problem was, later never came.

CHAPTER 18
WHERE IS
OLD MA KENSIE?

Nearly a week passed and the doorway of the *Oficina de Ventas* was still decidedly empty.

Where was Ma Kensie? She had wandered off before but never for more than a couple of days. Dolita was troubled. She knew something was wrong. She had searched all the usual places and asked everyone if they had seen the old woman. Ma Kensie was a well known character in the area, known to most people but no one had seen her for several days.

Returning to the shelter Mikey Mean tried to console her, he even offered to share one of his avocados, the latest stash under the mattress.

Dolita smiled at Mikey, a very forced, artificial smile and pulled her old blanket over her head.

No Ma Kensie! What possibly could be worse than this? She needed to know more, so many unanswered questions! Where was Raggy Man? He had wandered off too. Now this was getting too ridiculous to bear. Raggy gone again, she felt sure he would not be gone for long. Since her stay in the hospital he had always remained close by her side. Mmm….! Well Raggy would be back soon she was sure of that and she rolled over, snuggling under the blanket, oblivious to the outside world.

It was a restless night, perhaps one of the loneliest nights of her life, a warm clammy night. Suddenly she was startled by a noise and feeling a presence peered over the top of the blanket. There was One-eye staring at her inquisitively as if trying to strike up a conversation, meowing and purring as cats do! Was he trying to communicate with her? Well, she had not the slightest idea what he was saying.

Maybe One-eye missed Raggy Man too? Falling into a deep sleep, deeper than she had ever known before, something very strange began to happen.

She felt that she was floating, that her body was weightless and all the cares of the world had been lifted from her. The sky was blue, so truly blue it was breathtaking. Not a blot, not a blemish. It was as though she needed sunglasses yet there was no sign of the sun. Drifting more and more into the very depths of her dream the perfect blue engulfing her. Such an overwhelming feeling of peace and joy, then higher she went into the clouds soaring like an eagle. Not the dark rain clouds that she had often seen hanging low over the city, but white fluffy clouds. Their appearance was that of white candyfloss, whiter than white, the purest of white, so enchanting she felt that she wanted to throw herself around in them.

To jump and to slide. To tumble and to fall. It was heavenly, it was beautiful and she felt she wanted to stay there forever. Dolita saw the arch of a white rainbow. No, not a coloured rainbow! A white rainbow! It ascended higher and higher into the heavens and she wanted to climb it, to follow it to the rainbow's end. She began to mount it, clinging onto it's satin surface. Suddenly she found herself sliding down, it was an exhilarating and most intoxicating feeling. She wanted to shout out with joy and raise her arms, as if on a roller coaster she gasped with excitement. Then, a feeling that her insides and her very cheeks had been sucked out, with such pressure she felt that her whole body was about to explode at any moment. With a gentle thud the journey was over as she found herself back in her makeshift bed under her familiar dirty blanket. Daylight was breaking.

"Wow, One-eye" she whispered. "What was all that about? I would like to do that again," she giggled.

One-eye turned around and scurried away so fast she thought she had startled him but then realised that he had seen Raggy Man coming down the street.

Dolita squeezed Raggy Man in delight and then looking into his eyes she questioned, "Where 'av you been all night, are you up to mischief Raggy? Found a girlfriend or something? And where is Old Ma Kensie?"

She wished he had the answer to Ma Kensie's whereabouts at least.

She jumped to her feet, soon forgetting about the dream, dusted herself down and set off in her search once again, her faithful little dog by her side.

The sky was heavy, the air full of smog. The early morning sun trying to break through a gap in the clouds.

Together they would look for Ma Kensie. Today they would find her, she was sure of that. The search would begin again and they set off walking towards the *Calle Jeronimo*, crossing the *Avenida del Sol* in the direction of the *plaza*. Near the park, Dolita stopped for a while to watch the children and gather her thoughts. She knew some of the children who inhabited the park. Possibly one of them had seen Ma Kensie.

The children's play area was surrounded by blocks of flats mostly eight storeys high, all with narrow balconies.

Dolita looked up as the sound of chains and grating caught her attention. One of the *chicas* was extending the washing line which she drew on a pulley from one side of the narrow cobbled street to the other. Then, glancing towards the right of the street Dolita saw that Mariana was having another red day. In fact everyday was a "red day" for Mariana.

Pegging out her laundry every conceivable item was red. Different shades of red admittedly, but nevertheless red. Most weird! Most weird! What kind of a person wears nothing but red? Two rust-coloured T-shirts, a pair of scarlet, cropped trousers and a short, falu red skirt which looked more like a belt than a skirt. Other items of red, a cerise, satin baby-doll sleep suit and a collection of crimson lacy underwear.

"Drr...?" Manolo hated Mariana, he hated the colour red!

Dolita decided there were too many wacky people in the world and she was sure they all lived in her part of town.

Mariana Red, Mr. Twist, Dodgy Deuno, The Molina brothers, Bobby Sniff to mention but a few.

Mariana could only be described as a lady of the night. Rarely around during the day she could be seen standing on the corner of *Calle Inocente* most evenings. Quite a laugh, the name of the street meaning 'Street of the Innocents', hardly reflecting Mariana's personality. Standing expectantly, cigarette in mouth and always adorned in her favourite red outfit, so as to get noticed I suppose! Mariana would disappear with any character that thrust money into her hand, only to re-appear a couple of hours later to do the same thing all over again. What she did, Dolita didn't care to ask!

I am sure there was a time when Mariana had been considered attractive. Now she could only be described as "rough." This being somewhat of a kind description, having been called far worse by some of the local residents.

Dolita shouted across to Mariana who looked in her direction.

It was hard to distinguish whether she had two black eyes because someone had smacked her or if perhaps it was the make up and grime smudged from the night before. Mariana did mix with the most unsavoury characters and it would not have been the first time Dolita had seen her with a black eye.

"Seen Ma Kensie?" Dolita shouted across the street.

Marianna shook her hand and shrugged her shoulders indicating that she had not seen the old woman. Dolita disappointedly nodded in thanks and strolled on.

Finding a corner in the park near a selection of old tyres which had been put there for the little ones to play on, she watched the children as she tried to retrace the steps of the old woman. It did not make any sense to her. A person could not just disappear. Could they?

Well Ma Kensie had certainly done that. Just disappeared without a trace, what now?

The park was busy that morning and more than one person passed through on a cycle with a basket clipped to its frame. It was no rarity to see a dog in one of the baskets and Dolita laughed as a young woman cycled past with a tiny terrier in her basket. The terrier wore a small sun hat similar to a baseball cap and a tiny matching waistcoat. Dolita remembered the girl at the hotel and the tiny dog with the red feathery thing around its neck. For Heaven's sake what is it with people and their dogs? They're animals, why dress them up? Looking towards the terrier, sitting upright, his paws holding onto the basket, Dolita thought that had it not looked so comical it would have been sad.

Not that she didn't love animals, quite the contrary, her love of Raggy Man was proof of that. Her concern was that some people loved their pets more than other human beings. Kids were starving and animals were being pampered beyond ridiculous proportions.

"The balance is all wrong Raggy! What do you think? Want a cap and waistcoat?" she said and giggled heartily.

Raggy Man barked as though he understand every word she uttered.

Dolita's attention then turned to the children. Their happy little voices and the sound of their play rising above and beyond the parameters of the park. These children were happy, unlike the children she would see later that day, scavenging like dogs for food at the dump.

A little girl ran over to Dolita smiling cheekily, reaching out her petite grubby hand, as if asking her to go play. Dolita smiled but today she did not feel like playing. She was on a mission, a mission to find Ma Kensie. She nodded and smiled and the little girl ran off disappearing into a long rubber pipe which formed part of a very innovative maze of tunnels and passages, perfect for imaginative play. The pipes, some as long as 480cm with a diameter of about 96cm created an exciting and exploratory area for the little ones. The only problem being that unfortunately at night it also created a shelter for some of the homeless and the following morning some of the tunnels were found to be in an undesirable state if you know what I mean. The smell of the stale urine and glue substances would take a while to clear in the air, but the children seemed oblivious to the odours and played happily.

Most of these kids here had homes at least, many of them living in the surrounding flats and having the opportunity to go to school. Dolita wondered about school and reflected on the book she had taken from the house at 247. She looked forward to the day when someone would teach her how to read. Maybe she would even go to school! Unlikely but a nice thought. street kids didn't go to school! Of course not, they didn't exist. Ignored by many they were outcasts, an embarrassment. OK, provided they didn't hover around your doorstep. Well, perhaps she was being unreasonable. After all she was fortunate enough to have Alejandro and the Crisis team supporting her, and then there was Beeky, Deuno and Old Ma Kensie, she sighed...

Alejandro said there were around 240,000 kids living on the streets in *Distrito Federal*. This sounded like an awful lot of *chavos* to her. The nearest school, *Alajambre* Primary was just around the corner, Dolita had often heard their gleeful little voices at play. The school gates were locked when lessons began and they remained locked until the end of the school day. Security was stringent and the only access for pedestrians or delivery vans was first by way of contact with the school office. An intercom system built into the main school gates allowed everyone the opportunity to identify themselves before a pass was granted.

Dolita knew there would be no school today. It was Sunday and all the children would be home with their families, apart from the few local ones playing in the park that is.

A jogger passing by caught her glance. He was painfully thin with lanky legs and knobbly knees. His clothes were the same as those worn by the professional runners.

Lycra top and pants in cobalt blue with cerise pink stripes, he had a water bottle attached to a belt around his waist. Tuned into his personal walkman, he was taking no notice of anyone else in the park.

CHAPTER 19
THE SNATCH

L eaving the park, Dolita and Raggy set off in
the direction of the bazaar. A fashionable haunt
for both locals and tourists on Sundays.

There was a small, lawned square surrounded by
pretty gardens. It made a handsome park in the midst
of a busy commercial area. Scattered around the
square along the footpaths were the artists. Many
beautiful paintings in vibrant colours were hanging
on the park railings and strewn along the paths.

People strolled around, some just meandering with
no intention of buying. Others loved to barter for a
good price. The Indian girls who made the beaded
jewellery and fashioned the dolls had set up small
stalls alongside others selling handmade tablecloths
and napkins. Dolita had often seen them being made,
though she had no need of such things. She certainly
had never used a napkin in her life, nor was she ever
likely to. She loved the dolls which were essentially
made with coloured ribbon, beautiful colours and
so perfectly made. The reversible doll with the happy
and sad face amused her. Café bars surrounded the
bazaar and *mariachis* and other musicians began to
mingle among the crowds. Dolita watched as a
young girl passed amongst the crowd with a begging
bowl and a tiny baby straddled across her back, in a
carrier made of old cloth. She was ignored. The bells
could be heard softly ringing out, the locals exited

the church and began arriving to enjoy the atmosphere and take lunch after their morning prayers.

It was now nearing mid-afternoon and Raggy and Dolita were quite a distance from the shelter. It was dusty and she was thirsty and tired. "I think this is a hopeless task," whimpered Dolita. "How will we ever find Ma Kensie? She's gone, She's gone! I guess that's it. "Now I'll never find my mother. She's the only one who knew anything about her."

She hesitated and sighed, "Ma Kensie was special, Raggy. She loved us. I just know she did. She would never go away without saying goodbye. Something's happened to her. I feel it and I can't do anything about it. Come on Raggy, let's go home."

Together they weaved through the crowds milling around the market traders.

Suddenly a boy, mid-teens, pushed a seemingly frail old woman and she stumbled. Another boy coming from the opposite direction snatched her bag. "Team work," muttered Dolita and lunged forward to retrieve the bag. It all happened in a matter of a few moments and the boy from whom Dolita snatched the bag seemed more startled than the old woman. They darted off quickly whilst a big guy standing nearby who had witnessed part of the scenario waded in to help. He grabbed hold of Dolita and held her roughly.

"You scruffy little *escuincla*, give me that bag at once, you want a good hiding," he yelled, prising it from her grip.

"Ay, let go of the kid!" shouted a well-dressed, middle-aged woman who had witnessed everything.

172

She had seen exactly what was happening, and was angry to see an incident that nearly became a grave injustice. She screamed at the guy who was holding Dolita, aggressively. Shrugging his shoulders he backed off.

"Only trying to help," he snapped.

"Well, I saw the whole thing and the girl was trying to help too. "Those kids snatched the bag," she explained, pointing to the kids who were rapidly disappearing around the corner, "and the girl snatched it back."

"Uhm…. They're probably working together," he muttered.

"Don't think so, I live near these parts and I have seen those lads before, they're always up to no good."

Actually, she had seen them on numerous occasions and even pointed them out to one of the local *policía*.

Dolita handed the bag to the old woman whose stature was exceptionally thin and fragile. The whole fiasco had startled her and she looked anxiously at Dolita, managed a faint smile, and nodded her approval. The woman opened her bag and took out a piece of paper, pressing it into Dolita's hand.

Another observer, one of the traders, witnessing the commotion held out her hand to share her *chapulines*.

"Thanks, but no thanks," whispered Dolita. She had noted the kind gesture but was not into eating *chapulines*. High in protein, fried in chilli powder, onions and garlic. Sounds good eh! They were a Mexican delicacy, supposedly good with a squeeze of lime, but when all was said and done they were still fried grasshoppers.

Yuk! Not her thing.

"*¿Qué onda? ¿Qué onda?* In trouble again Dolita?" came a cheeky voice from behind. You certainly like to be where the action is, don't you?"

Dolita spun round and, as if he had appeared from nowhere, there was Pablo, the infamous Pablo Molina! Dolita caught his expression, he smiled, she blushed. He was wearing a neat pair of tight jeans and a short, cropped, black leather jacket. Dolita gave him a rather weak smile and was just about to move on, he took hold of her arm and motioned her to sit down.

"What's the rush?" he asked. "Let's hang around for a while, I've been wanting to talk to you for ages."

"What about?" asked Dolita curiously; she couldn't imagine what Pablo might possibly have to say to her. The bike incident had been long settled.

"What if I just like you?" said Pablo with a twinkle in his eye. "What if I just want us to be mates!"

"Can't imagine why," she said with a slight giggle, actually she did quite like him.

"I admire someone with guts like you Dolita, I've been watching you for a while. It takes courage to stand up to Maria Molina, and you must 'ave some bottle to rescue that little chiquita at the *basura*.

"I didn't stand up to Maria," said Dolita modestly, "it was really Bobby Sniff and Raggy who rescued me."

"Bobby Sniff I know, who's Raggy?"

Raggy felt dead proud, barked and wagged his tail. "Oh," laughed Pablo "and the *chiquita?*" "Anyone would have done the same in my position."

"Well I think you are one very special kid and I really feared for you, especially when you ended up in that hospital. Afraid you might die or something, that's why I sneaked in to check on you."

Dolita stood silently. Now she did want to sit down and perched on the kerbstone by the lamp post, Pablo sat beside her. Suddenly it all came back, the memories of the mysterious hospital visitor. As the sun broke through the clouds at that most opportune moment Pablo took off his black, leather bomber jacket, throwing it over his shoulders. She stared at him as he breathed deeply, puffing out his muscular chest, stretching the buttons on his bright-red waistcoat.

Dolita smiled and gently touching his arm whispered, "Thanks." They sat, side by side, suddenly neither knowing what to say, then, with a backwards glance, she signalled to Raggy and they strolled off.

Walking away, Raggy Man by her side she felt she had just found a new friend. Her knuckle clenched tightly, she released it unravelling the paper that the old woman had given her. Scruffy and dirty, it was a note. A 100 *peso* note. Wow! She had never seen one let alone held one. A 100 *peso* note!

Seemed like it was going to be a good day after all, yes, perhaps a very perfect day!

Dolita knew she had to give the money to Rocia or Enrique to buy food. This would buy plenty of food.

On the way back to the shelter she saw one of the street girls selling beaded bracelets, 10 *pesos* each. How she would love one. Stopping and hesitating for a while, she wondered…

No, certainly not! Any money they had needed to be used for food, not trinkets and trivialities. A nice thought, but no.

Besides, she would not dare to try to change the 100 *peso* note. No one would believe it was hers and someone was bound to try and take it from her. She decided to hurry back, momentarily forgetting about the search for Ma Kensie. She needed to find Rocia or Enrique quickly.

On returning to the shelter there was some kind of calamity with two of the younger boys, so Dolita left the money with Enrique and a full explanation of how she came by it, then raced off to find Angelina and Manolo, who had gone for a game of *fútbol*.

Amazingly, when the three of them returned it was to find Rocia embracing a large grin and cooking a huge pan of scrumptious looking vegetables and sauces.

Mmmm….! The aroma met them as they turned the corner. Rocia stirred the contents with a wooden ladle. She had really excelled! One Spanish onion, peeled and chopped, one red pepper, two long red chillies sliced with a sprig of thyme, four large roughly chopped tomatoes, a few garlic cloves and a selection of wholesome vegetables.

"When can we eat? When can we eat? "*Tengo mucha hambre*. I'm starving" mumbled Roberto.

"Five minutes," said Rocia who thrust a piece of uncooked *chayote* into his hand, thinking he really did look like he couldn't wait.

Filling some old plastic bowls she poured a generous portion into each one and passed the food to the kids, Roberto guzzled his food, making irritating noises. Dolita wolfed it down, as did the others. She then went and threw herself on one of the mattresses, thinking what an interesting day it had been. Raggy barked and picked something up off her dirty blanket.

"What is it Raggy?" she asked. He had a small, beaded bracelet in his mouth. Beautifully coloured and even prettier than those she had admired earlier.

"Oh, it's for you Dolita. Just a thank you for what you did for us all today. We have enough food to keep us going for a few days," said Rocia smiling.

"How extraordinary" Dolita thought, the curious expression on her face quickly turning to one of sheer delight.

Mulling over the day's events, thinking of Pablo Molina and examining the bracelet she puzzled.

How very, very extraordinary!

As it grew dark the kids settled down, satisfied and content, their bellies full, all having had a good "nosh."

Soon the shelter lay quite still but for the usual snores and the sound of Roberto's heavy breathing.

Dolita lay whispering with Angelina, discussing the day's events. Suddenly, the peace was disturbed by yet another commotion. There was never a dull moment in the lives of the street kids. Now Bozo was going crazy, some movement outside had certainly disturbed him.

"Oh no, don't say it's those filthy rats again," screamed Rocia, but soon realised that this was no rat, someone was snooping around outside. Well, she hoped it was human by the size of the shadow! Anything else didn't bear thinking about. Whatever it was it was creeping about on all fours and Bozo was not waiting to find out! He burst through the gap in the heavy tarpaulin cover and was gone. He sure was eager to protect the kids, and was soon encompassing the shadow, pinning it down, growling with such ferocity, it would have scared the pants off anyone. Indeed it did!

The shadow was none other than Bobby Sniff.

"Let him go, let him go!" yelled Dolita when she realised who it was. Finally and very reluctantly an angry Bozo backed off, allowing Bobby to dust himself down and scramble to his feet. A fine lot of gratitude that was he thought. Next time he would leave the intruder. See how they liked it then. He was only doing his job!

"Good boy," said Dolita flicking his ear later and patting the back of his neck when she realised what a wonderful guard dog he really was.

Well it just so happened that Bobby Sniff was already very delicate, Bozo pouncing on him in the middle of the night must have been a real fright and certainly didn't help matters. He was a big dog and although scrawny and underweight, he could tackle most intruders.

Rocia and Dolita got Bobby into the shelter. He smelled vile, a mixture of stale alcohol, urine and vomit: he looked even worse. Not much they could do to help him. He was working out something that he had obviously taken or "sniffed" as the case may be. He would have to sleep it off. Rocia ushered him into the shelter and he soon slumped in a corner fast asleep. When they all woke up the next morning he was gone! Nowhere to be seen.

CHAPTER 20
DANGEROUS DRIVING

The silent march organised by the Association of Victims of Violence started out peacefully but soon got out of hand when a few demonstrators turned violent themselves.

"Well that makes a lot of sense! There is always a demonstration about something in this crazy city," tutted Enrique. "What will they think of next? A demonstration against demonstrations I suppose."

Alejandro laughed. He was waiting to see the younger kids and had waded through the demonstrations to reach the shelter. Enrique had known there was something going down when he heard the police sirens and ambulance services in the distance. Alejandro sat down to have a game of cards with him.

"I might have to go back to the States soon," he said. "My mother is ill."

"Then you must go," replied Enrique.

"Yeah, but I don't like the idea of telling Dolita, that will be a tough one! Where are the kids anyway? They're out early!"

"No idea," replied Enrique. "What of Dolita, do you want me to tell her?"

"Of course not. When the time comes, if it comes to that, I will tell her. Probably won't be gone for long, and I sure wish I could get her settled into one of the *Hogares de Niños*."

"No chance of that!" exclaimed Enrique. "You will have to take all the kids. Dolita would never leave the others, the twins especially."

"I know," Alejandro said, just as Dolita crept into the shelter, a big cheeky grin on her face, carrying a huge pineapple. She threw her arms around Alejandro always thrilled to see her pal; after flinging the huge pineapple to Enrique who caught it first before it landed precariously on his groin.

At that moment there was an enormous crash, the screeching of brakes followed by a series of thuds, sounding alarmingly close.

"*¿Qué onda? ¿Qué onda?*" said Alejandro, looking very anxious. "What on earth was that?" A short silence and the kids all exchanged glances.

"I will go and check it out," he said, signaling Dolita and the others to stay in the shelter. Amidst the shouting and screaming the sound of sirens could be heard once more. Dolita was afraid and thought Alejandro was right. Alejandro could check this one out she had no intention of leaving the shelter.

Some time later Alejandro returned. Perhaps forty minutes had passed, it seemed more like four hours.

"Good thing you stayed here," he said, "not a pleasant sight."

"Go on then, what 'appened?" asked Dolita.

"Don't really know exactly, but they say a car hijack. Used for a robbery of some sort but the *policía* caught up with them. They were being tailed and took the corner too fast, skidded straight into a lamp post. The car a rather smart, black BMW was well and truly mangled, wrapped round a lamp post. It would have been an absolute miracle if the driver and the other passengers were alive. I didn't go too near, the *policia* had everything in hand, needed the fire brigade to cut them out."

"Oh how dreadful" said Enrique.

"Yeah, I can't stand those people who hang around accidents to see what's 'appened. It's gruesome. Glad I didn't see it," said Hugh listening to the conversation.

"Uhm…! Me too." agreed Dolita, Alejandro looked away knowing that Dolita would have freaked out if she had seen what really happened.

The idiots had not only used a stolen car in a getaway but had knocked over a kid who was standing on the corner of the *calle*, by the lamp post.

"Hope he's OK," said Enrique.

Alejandro didn't reply and kept his head down, he spent a couple of hours with the kids in the shelter. What they didn't know, but were to find out later that day, was that the kid was actually dead.

"He didn't stand a chance," said an onlooker who was describing the incident to Enrique later.

"The car came out of nowhere, driving like *locos* they were! Skidded on the hot, greasy road and the kid was just waiting to cross. What a tragedy, what a terrible, terrible tragedy."

"Put the word out. Find out who it is," said Enrique.

He did not have to wait long before the news came back.

* * *

Meanwhile, next day, Charlotte didn't intend to go out. She planned a quiet, restful day hoping to catch up on her paperwork and the heaps of information and articles that she had been given to read about Mexico D.F. A nice pot of English Breakfast tea: Twinings, the best! She settled down to read the daily paper. She decided to take a late breakfast, and a hearty one, then she wouldn't need lunch. Her feet and ankles were quite swollen so she thought it best to keep them elevated for a few hours. The city, known to have some of the world's worst air pollution from traffic and industry, had its problems intensified by the mountainous ring around it that prevented air from dispersing. That, added to the city's high altitude, caused an awful lack of oxygen. Hence, the headaches and nauseousness. Charlotte had certainly done lots of walking since arriving in the city and could guarantee without doubt a nauseous feeling and a rotten headache about mid-afternoon every day.

After working for a few hours and completing her journal, Charlotte decided to take a stroll near the hotel, before the evening rains came. The sky was already clouding over so she wouldn't go far. Perhaps to the kiosk around the corner for some chocolate. Yes, what a good idea! Suddenly she needed a chocolate fix.

The few hours rest had certainly helped the swelling in her feet and, slipping on some loose sandals, Charlotte left the hotel. Needless to say ten minutes later she was scurrying back, noticing the sudden wind that usually preceded the cloud burst, head down, munching a scrummy bar of chocolate and carrying yet another paper 'The Herald' an American paper which was easy reading. Sitting in the hotel lounge Charlotte ordered tea.

"What is it with the English and their tea?" laughed Benji, one of the most adorable waiters Charlotte had ever met. Settled down in a large squidgy armchair to catch up on the latest day's events, she read the headlines:

"More violence on the city streets as police chase ended in disaster."

The article continued : Three people were seriously hurt and a young boy killed as a police chase ended with a collision between a stolen vehicle and a lamppost at the corner of Calle Rual earlier today. A large quantity of narcotics were recovered from the vehicle including some small firearms and a list of addresses which officers of the AFI (Agencia Federal de Investigaciones) believe could lead to the arrest of several other drug traffickers in the city.

Ironically, although he has yet to be formally identified, it is thought that the dead boy is the youngest grandson of a well known drug baron.

Further details to be released later."

"How tragic," thought Charlotte turning to the report on the silent march of the demonstration of the Victims of Violence. She read how, sadly, that itself had turned violent. She threw the paper aside with an exasperated sigh, "What a crazy, crazy world we live in, what does God make of man's foolishness?"

"Did you say something Ma'am?" asked Benji clearing the next table. "No," replied Charlotte "just thinking aloud." Smiling awkwardly, she picked up some lighter reading.

* * *

In Cell 107, block C, East Wing, a prisoner shook his young friend, who was taking an afternoon power nap.

"Wake up pal, time for grub, if you miss it there's nothing else until 'morrow."

Tumbling out of the top bunk, he gave Enrie a friendly thump on the shoulder and the two of them left their cell. They edged their way to the front of the dinner queue. Enrie commanded the respect of everyone in block C, East Wing and no one was going to argue with him if he wanted first place in the prison canteen. Nicky joined them at their table in the far corner and the three of them wolfed down their chicken, beans, and chunk of bread. The conversation was non-existent, they were all too hungry.

Enrie broke the silence looking towards the skylight where a tiny sparrow had settled on the rusty iron bars. "I hate birds," he said.

"Why?" asked Nicky after a short pause. "Why, what's any little bird done to you?"

"I hate 'em, I really hate 'em! 'cos they're free!"

Silence fell again at the table and was only broken when a tap on the shoulder signalled that Enrie was summoned to the Governor's office. What could be going down, he wondered and followed the warden through the maze of badly-lit corridors and security points to the admin block. Even the admin block was oppressive and smelt stale.

Enrie was no longer considered a risk or a threat to security, although he was still in a maximum security prison. Twenty years served of a twenty five year sentence, he was due for parole and the authorities knew he was not going to do anything to jeopardise his freedom. He wanted out of there, and they knew it.

Enrie's life had been full of tragedy, violence and intrigue, having grown up a rebellious angry Puerto

Rican kid whose family had moved to Mexico City when he was eleven years old. He had escaped the arm of the law until his late forties; he was arrested and subsequently tried for various crimes including narcotics trafficking. Enrie was well respected in the underworld, feared and revered so to speak. He commanded that same respect in block C. East Wing, and it was well known among the inmates that he still controlled much of the

drugs trafficking in the city, although the authorities hadn't the slightest idea.

Now, there were several cases coming up for parole. Nicky and his cell mate, to name but two. Maybe that is why the Governor wanted to see him he thought. Yes! It must be about his forthcoming parole.

Enrie was a big guy, but the Governor was bigger. Walking into the office tall and lanky, towering over Enrie, he took a long lingering look at him. His face was thin and gaunt, his hair grey and receding. He certainly showed the stress of twenty years acting

Governor of one of the toughest penitentiaries in the Capital State. Yes, the two of them had done time together and Enrie had not always been so cool and relaxed. In those early days he had sure given Governor Toni Drabble some stick. Now the two men had mutual respect for each other and Enrie had settled many a prison dispute, riot and inmate feud, when Toni and his cronies did not have a clue where to begin. Toni was due to retire; Enrie decided that as soon as he was paroled, despite his age, his life was just about to begin. Of handsome stature, plenty of distinguished grey hair, good pecs and a muscular body, he was a fine specimen of a man. Working out daily with what little equipment was available to him he had maintained his fitness and certainly his appeal to the opposite sex. Ah! A woman, it had been a long time since he held a woman in his arms.

Enrie had enough money stashed away to last him the rest of his days and he had decided when he got out of block C, East Wing he was going straight. He was going to find his kids who were scattered in various parts of Mexico, rumours of some having gone over the border to the USA and be re-united with his long-lost family. What he most wanted to do was meet his grand-children. Maybe, find a new woman, his first wife having died in mysterious circumstances; he was going to settle down. Enrie was going straight!

"Sorry to be the bearer of bad news," said Governor Drabble, eyeballing Enrie and trying to look sympathetic.

"Molina, Pablo Molina, aged around twelve years," said Drabble. "I'm told he is your grandson," he hesitated, "killed in a tragic accident a few hours ago, thought you need to know, but then I don't suppose you ever met him, did you?"

Enrie looked at Drabble and the desire to smack him in the mouth for such a callous comment was overwhelming.

"No," he said. "I never did." Enrie's head bowed, a dark shadow of gloom covered his face. He felt numb, disappointed, angry and much, much more.

The warden escorted the subdued, pole-faced Enrie back to cell 107.

"What's up Molina?" shouted another inmate as he passed by his cell.

Enrie Molina did not answer.

CHAPTER 21
IN YOUR DREAMS!

That night Dolita felt sick - no Ma Kensie, Alejandro had told her he might be leaving and news reached her Pablo was dead! She rather liked him and thought that in time they may have become good mates. Dolita had made a point of finding out about him since he seemed to keep turning up in her life. She discovered that he was the youngest of several brothers and that his mother ran off with a gypsy years ago. His father's whereabouts were unknown. His grandfather, Enrie, was infamous, a leader of one of the cartels in Mexico trafficking drugs for years between Colombia and the States. A family rift, reasons unknown, had meant that Pablo's father and some of his uncles had broken off ties with his grandfather many years ago. Dolita discovered he was serving time somewhere on the Californian border. As for Pablo, she believed he wasn't a bad guy, and she didn't think he even knew about the stash in the handlebars. Oh what did that matter now! The Molinas were tough but Dolita thought Pablo was different. Not to say that he wasn't a tough cookie, but from their past conversations he was not into the organised crime and drug scene like his older brothers, not yet at least. Surely he didn't deserve to die like that and so young!

Yeah, the more she thought about it, the surer she was, her and Pablo Molina were heading for one special kind of friendship. Many of the kids went to his funeral, but she couldn't face it! Someone called Father Jose took the ceremony.

Dolita needed to think of something nice. Well she did and could be heard reciting the whole thing to the others the next morning.

"I was laying quietly and thinking about the Monarch butterflies," she said. "Anyway, I wondered how beautiful they must look and what an amazing sight it would be to see millions of

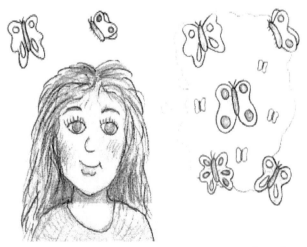

mariposas leaving Mexico all at the same time. How I wished I could see them."

"Erh…! What are you talking about, Dolita? *Mariposas*, what *mariposas*?" asked Manolo.

"Oh forget that," snapped Dolita. "Just something Alejandro told me. Listen, as I was saying, I was thinking about the butterflies when…"

"Yeah, the *mariposas*," squealed Manolo, laughing.

"Shut up!" snapped his sister, angrily, because he was making fun. She was all too anxious herself to hear about Dolita's latest *sueño*. Dolita always told Angelina about her dreams and either she truly had some amazing *sueños* or she had a vivid imagination. Whatever, Angelina loved to hear about them.

"Go on Dolita," she said, nudging her brother and giving him the 'sit-still-and-keep-your-mouth-shut' look.

"I know about the *mariposas*," mumbled Roberto. Everyone looked at him stunned. They thought he was sleeping and suddenly he was mumbling about Federal Officers guarding them.

"What! Are you *loco*?" said Manolo, laughing.

"It's true, it's true," he replied. "I heard it on the radio at the drug store."

"Heard what exactly?" asked Angelina curiously and momentarily forgetting about Dolita's dream.

"There are millions of 'em and they have set up road blocks to protect 'em."

"Now I know you are *loco*, squawked Manolo.

"Don't care whether you believe me or not. Some government guy said they should protect the butterflies, so they put up road blocks."

Now Dolita and Angelina looked at each other in absolute bewilderment: with puzzled expressions, they thought Roberto or someone had gone completely mad.

"How can road blocks protect them and from what?" asked Dolita.

"Illegal loggers." "Errrrr..?"

"They're chopping down the fir trees, selling the wood. That's where they stay from October until March. No fir trees, no butterflies, simple!" He could just imagine the fearsome axe and the fright of the butterflies leaving in their abundance as he began to simulate the action of the axe, throwing his arms about.

"Right," sighed Dolita looking fascinated but desperate to tell all about her dream.

A few seconds silence "… umm!"

Dolita continued. "Suddenly everything became really dark, quite black in fact as though there was no light anywhere to be seen. Neither above nor below, to the right nor to the left. It was pitch black and there was not a sound in the shelter. It was as though everything had stopped as though time had stood still."

"Oooh!" gasped Angelina, fixing her gaze on Dolita.

"And then they came."

"Who came?" asked Manolo. "Was it the *mariposas*?" he said mockingly, desperately trying not to laugh and holding his sides until he could bear it no longer and creased with hysteria, laughing like a hyena. Angelina smacked him where it really hurt.

"Shush *necio*! Listen you fool. Shush!"

"Don't call me a fool," grizzled Manolo."

"Well do be quiet then," said Angelina shaking her head and wrinkling her brow.

Dolita ignored them.

192

"The lights, the lights," she continued. "First one or two, then a few more and then there seemed to be thousands of them. They sort of came from one corner of the shelter, from the left I think. They began to fill one half of the shelter. First a few of them, then a few more until there were thousands."

"You said that once."

"Shush," said Angelina, "can't you see she is in shock or something."

Manolo howled with laughter.

Dolita went on, "It was most peculiar because they only filled one half of the shelter and the other half was still pitch black.

They formed a mass of twinkling, vibrant blue lights. They were brighter beyond bright, the colour too difficult to explain. The brightness dazzled and strained my eyes. They twinkled and shone as if they were flashing, thousands of times per second."

"Wow! Like before?" said Angelina.

"Yeah, just like the time I told you about when it happened before."

"And then what?" mumbled Roberto.

"Well it was as though there was a door."

"A door?"

"Uhm… What sort of door?"

"I don't know. A door. Sort of like a trap door I suppose you would say. Just above my head. Then I thought of the ants that I saw the other day. Just as an army of ants would follow their scout, so the lights seemed to turn their direction towards the door, gradually disappearing through it. Each taking its turn until the last one had disappeared. I felt as though time was standing still. An overwhelming feeling of peace washed over me"

"Wow! That's it?"

"Oh no, that is just the beginning. Listen to what happened next."

"You went through the door," skitted Manolo, thinking the whole thing sounded so utterly stupid, far-fetched and beyond all reason.

"I heard a voice, a strange voice which almost sounded musical, sort of like a trumpet. Follow me said the voice, come and see what I will show you. Suddenly I felt as though my body was being lifted up and in the distance I saw a rainbow, magnificent in colour. As my body moved towards the rainbow we passed beyond the clouds into an azure sky."

"What's that mean?" asked Roberto, puzzled.

"A perfect blue."

"How do you know such fancy words?" said Manolo smirking.

"Don't know. Just do."

Angelina glared at her brother telling him to be quiet and not interrupt again.

Dolita continued with the story.

"I saw an eagle. He was amazing and I watched him soar high above the clouds far into the heavens until I could see him no more." Dolita hesitated. "I know about eagles 'cos Ma Kensie told me about them. She said my great-great-great-great-grandfather or something, was called White Eagle and that he was an old Indian Warrior. She said he was named after the Eagle which was a mighty bird. They have excellent eyesight and…"

"Don't you know some stuff!" mumbled Roberto

"Mmm… suppose I do."

"So how?

"Just dooo…!" exclaimed Dolita, frustrated at the constant interruptions, wanting to get on with the story. "I watched the eagle. His wings were long and broad. He made a shrill high-pitched sound, then he zoomed down to what looked like a river and straight into the water. Then he soared high into the sky again. So high, with a large silver fish flapping in his talons." Angelina was captivated by the image.

"As I drew closer to the rainbow I could hear the most beautiful music. It was delightful, sweet and soothing and seemed to come from all corners of the Heavens. There were many different types of musical instruments playing. They made our *mariachi* bands sound so naff.

"Excuse me, I love the *mariachis*," said Angelina.

"Yes, me too, but this music was so different. I could also hear singing but it was in a strange language. Didn't understand a word of it!" she giggled. "Oh yeah, and guess what?"

"What?" came the reply.

"Everywhere seemed so bright and yet there was no sun. Can you believe it? There was no sun. The light radiated everywhere but there was no sun."

"You said that once," retorted Manolo. They all ignored him.

Dolita looked intently at the others and continued.

"As I was now moving more slowly towards the light it was a phenomenal sight. Everything I saw after that…" she hesitated. "… well, it was as though all the colours were exaggerated."

"What do you mean?" asked Manolo, trying desperately to look more serious.

"Well, I saw some baby rabbits playing and frolicking in the grass. They were so tame and one of them ran over to me. He was so sweet and so cute but guess what?"

"What?" the kids exclaimed together.

He looked at me curiously as if to ask who are you, where did you come from, then I noticed his eyes were different. Could not help but notice, it was so obvious really. He had one green eye and one pink eye."

"Uhm… weird!"

"No it really suited him. The pink eye was the prettiest pink I have ever seen, the green eye, a soft emerald green."

"More weird."

"His fur was immaculate, so smooth and pure snowy white. I moved towards him because I wanted to stroke him, I actually wanted to squeeze him, but he scampered away.

"I sat down for a while because I didn't know where I was or how to get back to the shelter. Part of me didn't care, I just wanted to stay in this beautiful place. When I looked up there was a man walking towards me. He was so pleased to see me and he had his arms outstretched in my direction as if to pick me up and swing me around. You know, like Enrique does sometimes."

"What's that buttercup? Heard my name," said Enrique just coming into the shelter. They caught each other's glance. She said nothing and, carrying

196

on with the story, Dolita went on to describe the grass and the flowers.

"It was like a perfect meadow. Every blade of grass was such a vibrant green, not like what we have 'ere."

"Dead, you mean," mumbled Roberto, looking outside the shelter at the surrounding areas.

"Yeah. No weeds, just beautiful green and then the flowers, wow! They were magical. The daffodils were enormous. The biggest daffodils I have ever seen and they were strange, like they were sort of lit up from inside. Do you know what I mean?"

"No," came the echo.

"Well, as though there was a light bulb inside each one of them, lighting them up."

Dolita hesitated, the others waiting expectantly, drooping jaws and staring eyes.

"Then I saw the *mariposas*, flying overhead just like the one Alejandro showed me.

"It was dead," chipped in Roberto, saracastically.

"Shush!" said Angelina.

"They were so beautiful and there were so many of them."

By now Angelina was truly mesmerised. Resting her chin on her hands she sat at Dolita's feet listening in absolute wonder and awe. She could have listened to Dolita's description of this amazing place for hours. Imagination or what, she wanted to hear more.

"Hey," said Roberto to some of the other kids who were just arriving back at the shelter.

"Dolita's had a *sueño*, another *sueño*, come and listen!

"What next?" asked Manolo, now listening intently, as interested as his sister.

"Tell me about the man," asked Angelina. "Who was he?"

"I don't know," replied Dolita, "before he reached me and before I could ask him I woke up back in the shelter." Her eyes glazed over. "Blast," she said.

After hesitating, "Oh well, I can tell you a little more at least. I heard the muffled voices of children in the distance. I knew them to be children of all ages. You know, the chuckles and giggles of the little ones and then the raucous laughter of the older ones. The voices became louder and then I saw them following behind the man. Like the Pied Piper."

"Who is he?" said a voice from the back.

"It's a story."

"Oh," he replied, a puzzled expression on the boy's face, still none the wiser. "So how 'av you heard of it?"

"Ma Kensie told me."

She continued, "The children passed me by and as they ran on ahead he disappeared from view. It was so strange because none of them noticed me. You would think I was not even there. I suppose they were all busy, sort of focussed on where they were going."

"Where were they going, do you think?"

"Well how do I know, *necio*…" she hesitated. "There were children of every nationality, tall ones, short ones, fat ones, thin ones, dark ones, fair ones, young ones and older ones.

Some of the older ones carried the little ones on their backs. They were like one big happy family. Do you know what I noticed most of all?"

"No," they all echoed together, gathered round her listening studiously.

"They were all dressed in white, each child wore the same, there were no 'designer labels', no signs of wear and tear. Their clothes were immaculate. Each child dressed in the purest of white linen with strands of gold thread woven through the material, there were no seams in the material, which was clearly of the utmost quality. Each child looking no less and no more than the other. Each child looked happy and so content. The faces of the little ones, especially, were shining like golden stars.

As the chattering faded and the quiet returned there was a faint whisper. "Dolita," said a voice and as I turned around there was one older boy who had returned. His face was familiar in some strange way."

Dolita pondered. "He reminded me of Bobby Sniff. He smiled at me, he was so happy, so contented. His face glowed and his eyes were wide and sparkly. What is more amazing, he knew my name, didn't he! Suddenly as if being summoned by one of the others, he turned and ran."

"What about the man? The man you said held his arms out, where did he go? Who was he?"

"I already told you that," replied Dolita, frustrated. "Listen, will you! I don't know. I woke up. Remember?" She carried on with the story describing everything so eloquently, she was in full flow and wanted to tell all.

"The river that I thought I had seen earlier, when I saw the eagle was as clear as crystal and on each side of the river were many trees. There were beautiful flowers growing out of the bark of one tree trunk and I heard in the distance a roar of rushing water, the whole landscape lit up. Two larger trees one on each side of the river were full of fruit. Lots of different types of fruit: so full that one tree was nearly bursting and it bowed with the weight. The river flowed in one direction into a great city, the city surrounded and protected by a high wall. Through the city the river flowed cascading down to the sea. It almost looked shallow in parts as though you could paddle in it, but I doubt that very much. An illusion I suspect. It became wider and deeper as it meandered towards the sea. I am sure no one would be able to cross it.

"I saw one of the gates to the city and the gate was shining as if it were made of the same stone that I have seen that rich woman wear. You know, the woman at the Gali-Gali Café Bar," she studied. "The one who has a necklace and matching earrings, just looked like the same stone."

"It's a pearl, the necklace I mean. It's a pearl," said Hugh.

"How can a gate be made of pearl? Err…" asked Roberto.

"Don't know," replied Dolita.

"I could see through one of the gates into the city and it was so gorgeous. Shining like a huge diamond and the streets looked as though they were paved with gold."

"You dreamer," said Manolo, laughing. The other children all gathered around listening intently to the tale. Dolita now had quite an audience.

"No really," she reiterated, seeing their expressions. "I'm sure they were made of gold."

"Well the whole thing sounds wacky to me," droned Manolo.

"You and your *sueños*, Dolita! At least you keep us entertained on a dull day."

Dolita looked hurt. She felt her bubble had just burst.

"Well it's a nice thought," chipped in Angelina.

"Imagine if there was a place like that, where every kid was happy. No poor kids. No rich kids. No have and have-not kids. Everyone equal. Mmm......! Sounds like Heaven to me!"

Silence fell in the shelter. A few seconds more and perfect silence. Mesmerized faces, puzzled expressions.

"Sorry, said Manolo, realizing he had been rather mean to Dolita. It's just that he didn't know what to make of her dreams, nor did the others.

Strangely, he thought, just maybe he was a little frightened. He loved Dolita so much and he didn't mean to tease her but he did think her imagination was a little wacky. If he didn't know better, he would say she was on something!

He leaned over and gave her a big squeeze.

"Sorry," he said again looking awkward. "Sorry for making fun."

"What is so interesting?" asked Rocia peeping into the shelter just at that precise moment when all was quiet, so quiet yet again you could have heard a pin drop.

"A dream, a dream, one of Dolita's *sueños*," said Angelina, now feeling quite dreamy and spaced out herself.

"*¡Qué chido!*" came a voice from the back of the shelter. "*¡Qué chido!*"

"Well scatter kids. Someone needs to find food around here and Raggy Man and Bozo could do with something to eat too."

Raggy Man and Bozo barked in unison. They knew and recognised the sound of the word 'food'. "Yeah," said Hugh "I'm starving. *¡Tengo mucha hambre!*"

Enrique looked on in bewilderment.

CHAPTER 22
THE STRANGE
ENCOUNTER

everal days passed and everyone forgot about Dolita's latest dream. It was Friday morning and Dolita slept late, the uproar and noise from the streets below had kept her awake most of the night. She leaned over and could see the twins were still there huddled together to keep warm, breathing deeply, they were fast asleep. They looked peaceful. She decided, as all was quiet, to look at her precious box and took it from its hideaway. She carefully opened it to display the contents:

A rather spectacular looking red feather, well preserved, with a mottled black fleck running through it.

A charcoal sketch of a girl about 15 or 16 years of age, now quite faded, a piece of tatty paper folded into four with the numbers 541342 written on it and the name Helga.

She pondered and then very carefully returned them for safe-keeping. Not that it was a secret hideaway. Everyone knew where the box was hidden, but the box and its contents were of no interest to anyone other than the young Dolita.

Dolita dusted herself down, put on her new shoes and stirred Raggy Man. She decided to go see Miggy, hopefully he would let her help with the shoe shine.

It was then that the twins raised their weary heads and said that they would walk with her.

Before going far they came upon a game of *fútbol* in one of the garden squares. Angelina loved *fútbol* if not more than Manolo. Dolita smiled, she wouldn't see them for the rest of the day that was for sure. As the other kids gathered from a few blocks away it would become more than a game, but a time of sharing and hanging out together, *chavos* being *chavos*.

Dolita found Miggy in his usual place, business was quiet so they sat and chatted for a while, she then strolled off and left Raggy who was, by now, fast asleep in one of Miggy's shoeshine boxes. She giggled, she didn't intend to go far, Raggy would soon catch up with her; she knew he would only have a short power nap. Her plan was to stay close to the *plaza* and she could hear the shouts and cheers of the *fútbol* game in the distance. Dolita walked towards the *Zócalo*, it was becoming a hive of activity.

One week before Mexico celebrated its *Dia de Independencia* and workmen were erecting flags and the decorations in preparation. The square was taking on the ambience of a real fiesta; the Mexican national colours - white, red and green - sparkled everywhere. *El Grito*, a day when Mexicans showed they were proud to be Mexican.

Here's just a quick history lesson:
When Christopher Columbus "discovered" America it opened the doors for many expeditions and the Spaniards set sail looking for gold and riches.

In the year 1521 they arrived in Mexico. Mexico at the time was a great empire built by the Aztecs, but the indigenous nations were oppressed by the Aztecs, and thinking they might have freedom under Spanish rule, they aided and supported the conquerors. Hence, the conquest of Mexico began, and for three centuries it was under Spanish rule.

During the early hours of 16 September, 1810 Father Hidalgo, a local priest, rang the bell in his tiny church; with the backing of a small group of supporters he called the people to fight for their liberty.

The 10-year War of Independence followed.

This moment is relived every year as the Mexicans remember and celebrate El Grito, the cry for freedom.

Dolita found a quiet spot and sat on the pavement. She glanced across the *plaza* watching the preparations and noticed a woman nearby who was looking in her direction. She took no particular notice at first and then became aware that the woman was walking towards her. To Dolita's surprise, she came and sat down on the pavement beside her. It was most unusual for someone, particularly looking as she did, to sit on a dirty footpath, and she clearly didn't care what other passers-by thought. One well-dressed woman, with a designer bag, looked at them and rebuffed as she passed by.

The woman sitting beside her seemed different to anyone Dolita had ever met. She was casually dressed but yet well dressed, *¡Muy elegante!* a phrase Dolita used to describe the rich women that she saw going into the grand hotels or taking lunch at the Gali-Gali Café Bar. The most striking thing about this stranger was her fair skin and blonde hair. A *güera*, as they would say in Mexico, a true *güera*! When she smiled it was as though her whole face shone like a fragrant flower and her eyes were bright and sparkly.

She was clearly foreign, certainly not from Mexico City. In fact, Dolita did not recall seeing anyone with such a fair complexion and golden blonde hair. Wait a minute, she pondered. She was rather like the woman that she saw in the office of the Procuraduría, the day her and Martinez took the baby. She faintly remembered stomping on her foot. Well, maybe not!

The woman spoke to Dolita and asked her name. Dolita ignored her and the woman sat quietly for a while and then, smiling, asked again.

"Don't talk to strangers!" snapped Dolita, rubbing her dirty face and throwing back her matted hair.

"That's good," remarked the woman, "quite right too. I teach all my children that."

Dolita was now feeling rather disgruntled. Who was this foreigner suggesting she was a child? Indeed! How dare she! Just about to get up and move on something stilled her. Hesitating for a moment, Dolita was grateful when the stranger produced a cheese and ham panini and seemed willing to share it. Being very hungry that day suddenly the stranger had her full and undivided attention. The conversation then flourished, seemingly the stranger's name was Charlotte and Dolita's gut instinct soon told her she was OK. Charlotte was ordinary and very natural, obviously an intelligent woman but yet very childlike in other ways. She was so bubbly it was as though her bubbliness frothed over and was intoxicating. This woman was different to anyone she had ever met before and whatever she had Dolita knew she wanted some of it.

As they chatted, oblivious to the activities in the square, they never noticed a group of Zapotec Indians in full warfare regalia who proceeded to perform for some local tourists.

Charlotte tried to speak Spanish and made Dolita laugh because her words came out all confused. Her native language was actually English. Well at least she knew enough Spanish that they managed to communicate.

"Suficiente para sobrevivir," said Charlotte.

Dolita couldn't speak any English other than the few words that Enrique had taught her, which amounted to basically, "yes," "no" and "get stuffed."

"Where is England?" asked Dolita, having absolutely no idea. She had never been out of Mexico City. In fact Dolita only knew her part of town and had no idea of the full expanse of the city or indeed the grandeur of Mexico itself. Dolita had heard people talk about the delicious coast, the breathtaking *pueblos* and superb mountain ranges, it meant nothing to her. England certainly meant nothing to her. She had never watched television and knew little or nothing about other parts of the world. Dolita's education was limited to survival on the streets.

"So where is England?" she asked again, shrugging her shoulders. Charlotte proceeded to explain that it was approximately 10 or 11 hours *por* avión, depending on wind speed.

"Wow!" gasped Dolita, who could not really gauge 10 or 11 hours on a plane until Charlotte explained in street terms.

"About a whole day from waking up mid-morning to crashing out late evening."

Now Dolita understood that. She certainly didn't like the thought of going to England, not that there was any likelihood of that. Ugh….! Imagine having to sit still for 11 hours. Impossible for her but she supposed Roberto could manage such a trip since he spent most of his time sleeping, he would just sleep all the way there! She decided if anyone ever asked her to go to England she would send Roberto in her place. As if!

"So what you doing in Mexico?" asked Dolita.

Charlotte laughed. "Oh that is a long story!"

"Try me! Nothing else to do today. May as well listen to you," she giggled becoming more fascinated by the *güera*.

Charlotte said she had worked with children for many years and also had children of her own but they were now quite grown up. She told her about her heart to help the street children. Surprisingly, they also talked about Dolita's mum, how she missed having a mum, though she hardly remembered her, and that she hoped to see her one day soon. Dolita was quite forthcoming with the stranger and not at all withdrawn as one might expect. She told Charlotte about her dreams and she listened with interest.

"I don't always understand my dreams!" exclaimed Dolita. "The other kids just laugh and make fun of me, they say I am a dreamer and have a vivid and wild imagination. Roberto says I know too much."

"And how's that?" asked Charlotte. "Don't know, just do!"

"Perhaps one day Dolita, you will be able to tell me about some of your dreams, maybe I will be able to make sense of them for you."

"Stupid woman!" she thought. "How could this woman, who was not even from Mexico City and did not live on the streets, begin to understand her, let alone interpret her dreams?

"I, too, have dreams," said Charlotte.

"About what?" exclaimed Dolita, studying for a while and wondering what she could possibly want. I bet she never dreamt about where her next meal was coming from or finding her mum. "Uhm!" Thinking carefully about Charlotte's words, now she was really puzzled. She probably had everything!

Charlotte laughed.

"Maybe I dream about meeting lots of Dolitas and helping at least some of them find their mums."

"Oh, very twee," said Dolita sarcastically but then shuddered, a small glimmer of hope transparent on her face. "Does that mean one day you will help me find my mum?" she asked. "Besides, Old Ma Kensie said there is only one Dolita!"

"Who is Ma Kensie?"

Her words felt as she imagined one of her grandfather's swift arrows might feel as it found its mark, remembering how much the old beggar woman meant to her. She fought back the tears.

"An old friend," she replied abruptly, fidgeting, clenching her fists and shifting position.

Charlotte, recognising she had touched a sensitive spot, changed the subject quickly.

"Of course, there are no two people alike, God made us all different."

"Uhm…!" shrugged Dolita. "Do you think you could help me find my mum?"

"No promises that I can't keep, but I have one suggestion."

"What's that?" "Hold onto your dreams, Dolita, because you've got to have a dream. if you don't have a dream, how you gonna have a dream come true?

"Sounds like a song." "It was!"

"What?"

Charlotte laughed.

"Write down your dreams, everything has an appointed time.

"Whaaat…? Are you joking? I can't write!"

"Well perhaps someone can write them down for you until you can write."

"Charlotte, would you teach me to write?"

Charlotte laughed. "One thing at a time, young lady! I'm only here for a while and then I have to return to England."

"Blast! Another friendship not meant to be! Well, nice thought."

Raggy ran over, startling Charlotte. He had been curled up nearby watching the pair of them and now it was time to make his presence known. Dolita enveloped him in a gigantic hug.

Dolita was now getting fidgety. It was time to go. The pair of them had certainly bonded and aroused the attention of passers-by. Charlotte looked into Dolita's dirty little round face and thought of the *Oficina de la Procuraduría*. Maybe...? She hesitated then stood up, rubbing her aching back. Sitting on a pavement slab for a couple of hours, was not the most comfortable of places.

She looked down at Raggy Man. "What an adorable little dog," she thought. Dolita giggled and was just about to run off when the most extraordinary thing happened.

Charlotte said that she would like to give Dolita a gift and she reached into her bag, pulling out a doll, the most amazing doll Dolita had ever seen.

She was truly beautiful. Like a rag doll, the most beautiful doll she had ever seen. Her legs were long and slender. Her body slim, she had a pretty round face, with freckles around and above her nose.

Her clothes were vibrant, the colours captivating. She wore a plain bright red t-shirt and striped dungarees. The diagonal stripes looked as though all the colours of the rainbow had been taken and carefully sewn into them forming each vibrant stripe. Red and yellow and pink and green, orange and violet and blue. The colours were so passionate, so strong. On her feet she wore black satin boots with pretty laces and on her head a baseball cap, plain but inscribed with the initial "R" in the centre of the peak. Her hair was long, exceptionally long and perfectly plaited in two pigtails which fell below her waist. A thin strip of scarlet red ribbon was tied at the end of each plait. Finally she had a petite, scarlet purse with a long thin shoulder strap which she wore over her right shoulder and which rested on her left hip.

She was the doll of her dreams.

Dolita gasped. She could feel the goose-bumps all over her body. She could hardly catch her breath. How could this be?

Unbelievable, unreal, surreal! The words 'how can this be?' whirling round and round in her head, like a scratched CD, spinning over the same line. It was spooky.

Dolita clutched the doll tight to her body. Trying to fight back the tears and then, she wept, but this time, they were tears of joy. She was so overwhelmed that she quickly agreed to Charlotte's suggestion to meet at the same place, same time, next day. Off she went as fast as her legs could carry her, running with such speed she thought her legs were going to part from her body. Her heart was beating rapidly and racing back to see the others she practically tumbled over One-eye and Raggy Man who had returned to the shelter before her. She hurled herself into the shelter with the fury of a great tidal wave.

"My goodness girl, *¿qué onda, qué onda?*" shouted Rocia. "Whatever has happened to you?"

"The dream, the dream. It's the dream!"

"Slow down Dolita you will burst a blood vessel." By now all the others were gathering to see what event had prompted such a stir. Raggy Man and One-eye kept discreetly out of the way to avoid being kicked or trampled on in the excitement. Even Pygmy came out of his nest to see what was going on.

"It's the dream," shrieked Dolita, almost hyperventilating, feeling as though her insides were going to explode at any moment.

"Now slow down," Rocia cried, taking hold of Dolita's hand, eye-balling her with a calming manner.

"Take a deep breath and then speak slowly. Now what happened? *¿Qué onda?*"

Dolita, stunned by what had happened and still reeling from the shock, took a deep breath and began to tell the others about the amazing encounter.

"I met this *güera*," she blurted out. "Her name was Charlotte. She gave me this," and held up the doll to show them. As she did Angelina and Manolo arrived. Now it was Angelina's turn to shriek. She knew quite well about the doll in Dolita's dream.

"Oh buzzing! I'll eat my cap! Dolita, it's the doll in your dream, the one you told me about when you were in the hospital. Wow!"

"You don't have a cap," laughed Manolo, "you lost it, remember?"

Angelina glared at him and elbowed him in the chest. Sometimes her brother was so infuriating. The excitement in the shelter that night soon became too much to contain. Noise was an understatement as the kids enthused. The chatter and the questions could be heard until the early hours. How can this be? Who is this Charlotte? And how did she get a doll exactly like the one in Dolita's dream?"

Weird, weird, very, very weird!

Dolita fell asleep, clutching the doll and wondering if when she woke she would still have it, or was this simply, yet another dream? She slept for hours, she was exhausted. When she finally woke, there she was the doll of her dreams, lying beside her. It was true. It really did happen.

Just about to wake the twins who were sleeping soundly, curled up together beside her, an awful thought crossed her mind. She had agreed to meet Charlotte and had slept so long she would probably have missed her.

She didn't have a watch: if she had it would be no use to her as no one had ever taught her to tell the time. Deciding to go alone, slipping quietly out of the shelter and clambering down the slope at the side of the metro station, off she went. She could tell by the activities in the street that it was mid-afternoon. The market traders were just beginning to clear away and the smells of the lunchtime snacks were fading. A shout startled her and as she turned around there were her friends, Manolo and Angelina running towards her. Raggy Man followed quickly at their heels. Dolita knew that it was most unlike her to set off on an adventure without Raggy Man, but she had been so pre-occupied with the thought of missing Charlotte.

"Sorry Raggy Man," she said, tweaking his ear and smiling at the twins, glad that her best friends were with her.

"OK," chortled Angelina. "Let's go and find your *güera*!"

Half an hour later Dolita and the twins arrived at the very place where she had met Charlotte the day before. There was no one there.

"Are you sure this is the place?" questioned Angelina.

"Of course I am sure."

"How do you know?"

"Just do!" snapped Dolita angrily thinking that she had missed her new friend.

Half an hour passed, then another half hour.

"Come on," urged Manolo, "I'm out of here. You coming, Angelina?"

"No, I'm going to wait a while longer with Dolita," she said, seeing disappointment and emptiness written all over her friend's face. Actually, Angelina was disappointed too. She wanted to meet the *güera*.

Looking around the square the preparations were still in hand. The kids were watching the commotion as the erection of a framework for an outside stage to host the *Grito* celebrations collapsed. A gasp from the crowd and a sudden tap on the shoulder, the startled Dolita spun round to see the smiling face of Charlotte.

With a sigh of relief the two kids found somewhere to sit with her and spent the next hour chatting.

Charlotte had some delicious provisions in her bag and they ate as they talked. Some freshly-cooked croissants, slices of ham, cheese, some tiny sausages and pieces of *chorizo*, all neatly wrapped in napkins. Obviously smuggled out from the breakfast table, two large ripe bananas and a kiwi finished off the feast.

Charlotte saw the kids a few times during the following week and she also visited their habitat, which of course was the shelter. Would you believe she had a game of cards with them! Of course Mikey Mean won, as he always did, these days though he seemed to be winning honestly, without cheating! Coincidently, this was one of the places she had visited with the guys from the Crisis Team. Funny, she had not seen Dolita or any of the girls at the time.

CHAPTER 23
EL GRITO

The day of *El Grito* arrived. It was 8.30 in the evening and the crowds were flocking to the *Zócalo*.

"*¡Vamos a ver!*" said Enrique, "let's go and join in!"

An excited whisper passed around the shelter and without further ado the twins, Dolita, Roberto, Enrique and Hugh were on their way. The younger ones would certainly not have gone alone but they felt very safe with Enrique and Hugh overshadowing them.

The streets would have been very dangerous at that time of night, for the young ones and so far away from home! Dolita knew of gangs who enticed young kids with the promise of food, and then freely gave them drugs, only to abuse their bodies. Thank God she had never met any such person! As they began to get nearer to the great *plaza* the noisemakers could be heard in the distance: the whistles, the shakers and the false trumpets. Flag merchants gathered around selling all types of Mexican flags. Finally, they turned the corner to see the roads barricaded and strict security controls on each corner, *hombres* queuing one side, *mujeres* and girls the other.

"We have no chance of getting through," exclaimed Angelina. "A few scruffy *chavos*. I don't think so!"

First they had to run the gauntlet so to speak. The streets were lined with youths carrying confetti, cans of crazy foam and aerosols with sticky, green goo, anything designed to spray and be messy. By the time they reached the barriers even the best-dressed people were looking wet, bedraggled and decidedly untidy. It was hard to tell the best from the roughest apart.

Enrique ushered Dolita and Angelina along with a crowd of older women.

"Stick with them," he said, "keep walking and I will meet you on the other side."

"Ooooh... that helps," giggled Dolita and squeezing Angelina's arm, off they went.

Keeping their heads down so as not to get a face full of crazy foam, they kept close to the women who, by now, all looked as though they had had a bad hair day.

Before they knew it, they were past the barriers.

"Whew," said Angelina, looking round in a panic for Enrique and Hugh.

"What if they don't let them through?" she asked
"They will."

"How do you know?"

"Just do," said Dolita, a big sigh of relief and a chuckle as she saw Enrique walking towards her.

"Am I glad to see you!" she said, slipping her petite little hand into his.

Now Dolita was not into holding hands but today she would make an exception. There were thousands of people milling around the square and she was determined not to let go of Enrique. As the evening advanced the crowds kept increasing and the euphoria, the excitement and the tension were breathtaking.

They somehow seemed to get separated from Hugh, Manolo, Roberto and Angelina so she squeezed Enrique's hand even tighter.

"Hey," said Enrique, "steady on, you sure have a tight grip, I won't lose you." He laughed loudly, putting his strong muscular arms around her in a reassuring manner, sheltering her from the pressing crowd.

The outdoor stage which Dolita had seen them erecting earlier in the week housed the main entertainment, while the President and his entourage made their grand entrance on the opposite side of the square and disappeared into the Royal Palace. They marvelled at the enormous flag towering above the buildings, magnificent in its splendour. Throughout history it had registered diverse changes but in 1821 the current flag was adopted - its three colours, green  for independence, white for purity and featuring the national eagle in red for union. Other huge banners, ribbons and bunting were straddled across the buildings. The entertainment was terrific and Dolita experienced the most momentous night of her life. It was truly a night when she felt proud to be Mexican, even though she was only a street kid, homeless and despised by many. Tonight she was Mexican through and through and when the President appeared at the climax of the evening on that ever-so-royal balcony, the cheer went up, the *Grito* cry.

"*¡Viva México! ¡Viva México! ¡Viva México!*"

Dolita was so overwhelmed she never uttered a word. The atmosphere was electric. In excess of 40,000 people mimicking that cry to freedom all those years ago. It was breathtaking, sound waves rocked the square; suddenly a barrage of multi-coloured rockets hit the sky. A firework display beyond description and absolute delight on the faces of the onlookers, the glee experienced by the children. This was truly a night to remember.

The festivities coming to a close, suddenly she felt a surge as the huge mass of people all began to try and exit the square at the same time. This was scary! Dangerous, stupid or what?

Worse than an exit from the world's biggest football match they were swept along a tidal wave of people. Dolita began to feel the breath leaving her body as she gasped, sandwiched from all sides.

Enrique's big strong arms around her once again she still felt vulnerable. They couldn't stop, they couldn't turn to the right or the left, there was nothing to do but keep walking for what seemed like an eternity. Pushed along, finally the narrow streets leading off from the *zócalo* began to widen and other adjoining avenues merging, allowed the crowd to disperse.

"Thank goodness for that," sighed Dolita. "That was hairy!"

Enrique had to admit he had not been too happy himself and then to their utter amazement, Hugh, Angelina and the others turned the corner.

"Well that's one big coincidence, you startled me!" exclaimed Hugh. "All these people and we should find you two again!"

They all laughed.

"Don't hang around," ordered Enrique, "It's well past midnight and we have to cross the worst part of town."

A car pulled alongside them and two foul-looking guys peered through the windows.

"*Padrotes*," said Enrique, "thank God there's safety in numbers." Darting across the road the kids made record time and hiked it back to the shelter.

* * *

A few days later and Charlotte leaned back in the comfortable seat.

Writing in her journal the entry was:

Day 21. 24th September

A little piece of my heart will always remain in Mexico. Seen the beauty, the magnificence of such an amazing city and its people, but also seen the pain and the abject poverty of the poor. The plight of the street children has touched my heart so. As for the abandoned babies my heart grieves...

"Did you like Mexico?" asked the steward, as he offered Charlotte a soft, cosy, tartan blanket and a small, fluffy, white pillow to enhance her comfort on the journey home. It was nearly midnight and the cabin lights were dimmed for take-off.

Her eyes engaged with his as she layed her journal aside. She smiled and nodded as he was called away to assist an elderly lady who seemed to be confused about where she was supposed to be seated. As the huge Boeing gained height she looked out of the window. A mirage of millions of twinkling tiny lights: Mexico City by night. Surely this was the most awesome sight she had ever seen.

She thought of the street kids, the *chavos* as they called themselves. She thought of that momentous night *El Grito*, when she had gone to the *Zócalo* and joined in those famous celebrations. She remembered feeling uncomfortable and thinking she must have been the only blonde there.

"Keep your cap on," laughed her escort. She had felt vulnerable but at the same time safe, escorted by the Major, the man who had invited her to the celebrations, and an absolute gentleman he was too! The only thing that had worried her was the mass exodus just after midnight when a huge surge of people all tried to leave the *Zócalo* at the same time. What a night that was and she had forgotten to tell Dolita.

She thought of Dolita. Her heart ached.

She would go back. In God's timing she would go back to Mexico D.F., of that she was sure.

"Can I get you a drink Ma'am?" asked the steward, returning to her assistance.

"No thanks. Well, perhaps a drop of water!

"You were saying" he asked.

"Excuse me?"

"About Mexico?"

"Oh, *¡conocerlo es amarlo!*" she said and laughed. The steward clearly had no idea what she meant. "Knowing it is loving it," said Charlotte dreamily.

She closed her eyes and fell asleep.

Below, Dolita felt the nip of the night air. She sat alone at the entrance to the shelter; all was quiet within. Strangely enough not a sound could be heard, other than the hype as a local cantina spilled out its contents. Suddenly she was distracted by the sound of a solitary bird in the night sky, a sparrowhawk, he caught her attention as he dived towards the shelter.

She studied him as he moved restlessly from pillar to post and then soared and vanished. As she turned her eyes away, she faintly heard the sound of the jet and, had she looked, she would have seen its magnificent shape outlined in the murky grey sky. It gathered speed, leaving the city, magnificent in its splendour, 25 thousand feet and climbing; a grating sound shook the heavens as its wheels retracted and it was gone, no longer to be seen by the prying eyes of the city below. Its passengers? Of differing nationalities, they were settling down for the long 10-hour trek back to England.

* * *

Dolita pulled the old threadbare blanket over her legs. She liked it, it used to belong to Old Ma Kensie. She closed her eyes and fell asleep, the warmth of Raggy Man's body snuggled up by her side.

CHAPTER 24
EMPTY DAYS

The weeks passed by, life on the streets continued. Charlotte had left on the 24th of September. Alejandro left on the 24th of October.

Oh, Dolita had been forewarned but still hoped that it would not happen. She could hardly blame Alejandro. She would be on a plane too if her mother needed her, "too true": the chance would be a fine thing. But his mother was recovering from an illness and that was not the reason for his departure. Dolita recalled the moment when he had told her.

"There is something I have to tell you," he said

Dolita could see the alarm in his face and suddenly as if by intuition, she knew what he was going to say.

"I have to return to the States, I want to continue my studies." She didn't hear any more. She didn't hear him say when he was going. It didn't matter, next week, next month. She couldn't bear to lose another friend. It had now been several weeks since Ma Kensie disappeared; Dolita missed her dreadfully.

She had begun to trust Alejandro and since Ma Kensie's disappearance so looked forward to his visits to the shelter. He knew so much stuff and was so sweet, he even helped her to read a little, and write her name. He had tried especially hard to get her off the streets, but she was accustomed to it.

Having none of it, she was one of the Street Kid Gang, the streets were in her veins, whether she wanted it or not, street life was truly in her veins. Enough, she thought. No more! If Alejandro was going away, well, he just may as well go, it didn't matter when. She would not see him again! She felt hurt, she felt betrayed. She felt angry. She stood up and furiously kicked over the barrel of dirty water, which they had used to wash their clothes earlier. Wetting Alejandro through, she looked at him angrily and stomped off.

Why, oh why, was life full of broken promises?

Why, oh why, did everyone let her down? What was life all about anyway? Was there no hope for the future?

At the shelter that day Dolita refused to speak to anyone. She didn't care that Angelina had 17 mosquito bites on her legs and was going potty with the itching. She didn't care that One-eye had caught a baby *conejo* and dragged it helplessly into the shelter and was just about to eat it. She didn't care that Miggy could not find his only perfect shoe shine brush and that Rocia had no food.

She didn't care! She didn't care! She didn't care!

Sitting quietly alone she held her precious doll and taking the box that she had saved from the house at 247, she once again examined its contents. Tracing her fingers over the outline of the beautiful young woman in the faded sketch she wondered who she was. The tatty piece of paper with the numbers 541342 and the name Helga. Who was Helga? And finally, the vibrant red feather with the mottled black fleck. Mysterious, very mysterious but a mystery she would solve one day.

Drawing her blanket over her head, Raggy snuggled beside her. They slept soundly waking to the sounds of a new morning.

Four weeks to go and the city was preparing for Christmas. It was a pleasant day and the weather was mild. The bars and restaurants on the fringes of the city's squares were great for the pastime known as "people watching" and this is exactly how Dolita spent much of her time doing just that, "people watching". Sneaking quietly un-noticed out of the shelter, shaking Raggy to go with her, after aimlessly wondering around, she found herself sitting on the wall by a fountain, almost hidden among the shrubs. It was a shady spot in a leafy corner, one of her favourite haunts. There, no one noticed her.

The high-backed chairs and decorative tables gave the square a touristy ambience. But there was not a tourist in sight, it was full of locals. She knew, you could tell the foreigners and tourists a mile away. *Gringos*, they often called them.

It was actually a very unusual looking café bar. Some might describe the décor as rather zany but its character attracted the punters in droves, not to mention the delicious aromas of exquisite and scrumptious cuisine. The colour scheme was pink and yellow, blue and orange, alternating. Let me explain.

The furniture being made of wood comprised oblong tables, each with four high-backed chairs. To accommodate larger groups two tables were pushed together.

226

OK, so orange table = pink chair next to blue chair next to yellow chair next to orange.

Blue table = orange chair next to pink chair next to yellow chair next to blue. Get it?

Never were two chairs the same colour placed together. The colours of the tables varied. Then just to add a little more colour as if that were not enough, the parasols were... guess what?

Pink, yellow, blue and orange striped.

This was the Gali-Gali Café Bar.

Interesting, Eh?

Dolita watched the man sitting alone in the corner who was irritatingly loud.

"He is *loco*," said one of the waiters, "completely mad," and each waiter in turn ignored him as they carried on with their duties. The *loco* seemed to be oblivious to the fact that he was being ignored and continued to laugh and chatter to people around him. Finally his presence became a nuisance and a rather well-dressed guy, probably the café bar owner, appeared from nowhere and moved him on. Shouting and waving his arms in frenzy, like someone who was demon-possessed, the man was adamant that he was not going quietly. He viciously kicked over a nearby ceramic planter, spreading its contents all over the cobbled square, shrugged his shoulders and reluctantly left.

All quietened down apart from the usual bustle of the café bar until the office workers began to leave their work places flooding into the square for lunch.

The waiters were now certainly too busy to notice Dolita who loved to sit discreetly in her favourite spot and see how the rest of the world lived. Women in trouser suits with fancy handbags. Men with polished shoes and designer shirts.

There was something very peaceful about this place.

The sound of the water cascading down the four tiny fountains behind her. She loved most of all the little sparrows which filled the square. She watched them taking pleasure in their activities, singing and chirping as if without a care in the world. So tame they would sit beside her, eagerly hopping between the tables.

They were becoming more daring each time she saw them and she sat and beamed as one little sparrow leapt onto a high-backed chair and rested a while. Then skipping onto the next empty table he picked up a chunk of bread and scarpered fast. Very pleased with himself he was too! Dolita giggled, how she loved those little sparrows.

People continued to order drinks and food as her eyes focused on one woman in particular, the woman seemed familiar, Dolita had seen her before. She was very elegant, most debonair. She arrived with a striking, well-built man; probably her driver because many of the lady's had chauffeurs or someone to drive them around the city. He left after they both synchronised their watches, it appeared as though they had agreed a time for his return. Clearly older than the rest of the people in her group, her appearance oozed wealth. Black sleek hair scraped tightly away from her face and fastened with a very exotic Spanish comb. The sort the Flamenco dancers wore.

Dolita had seen a display of Flamenco dancing at a street festival, and it was quite different to Mexican dancing. She loved all music and dance but most of all she loved to listen to the *mariachi* music. She was delighted when a group of *mariachis* began singing nearby and she watched as one of the musicians walked over to the woman to serenade her. The woman pressed some coins into the hand of one of the musicians and they sang again before moving on.

Dolita studied the woman who wore a black lightweight sweater with a black and white knitted, interwoven wrap draped over her shoulders. The effect was stunning.

Her neck and wrists were adorned with white pearls and a lady of such grandeur obviously had the earrings to match. She had high cheekbones, a clear but well powdered complexion and wore bright red lipstick, which perfectly matched her long painted fingernails. Rings on each finger she clasped the hand of a colleague just arriving and he leaned forward to kiss her on each cheek.

Dolita was amused that where her eyebrows were meant to be it was as though she had shaved them off and had drawn a thin black pencil line.

As the food began to arrive and the strong smell of garlic and freshly baked bread drifted past her nostrils, it was time to move on. She couldn't bear the thought of watching them eat.

By now the square was buzzing with the sound of the *mariachi* music. Several other groups of musicians had turned up and the square boasted a real festive spirit. Each group was colour coordinated in silver, royal blue and scarlet outfits with silver-studded, wide brimmed hats. They did look quite spectacular. The sound of the *mariachi* music, a pleasure to her ears, the songs usually telling a story of love, betrayal or heroism.

Perhaps they should tell the story of the street kids, she thought and moved on.

She strolled down the nearby narrow cobblestone passageway flanked by adobe walls and walked through the historic quarter, the oldest area in the city. She passed a grand property and was able to catch a glimpse inside the grounds of one of Mexico's most gorgeous and elaborate homes, before the electronic gates closed.

Crossing more narrow and ancient streets, it would have been a pleasant ramble for wandering tourists but for Dolita it was a drudge.

She passed through an area inhabited by the poorest of the poor. Nearing a busy traffic inter-change, the contrast of the busy square where people spent freely and the abject poverty of the city's poor became evident. She watched as a youngster jumped almost on the oncoming car bonnet with little or no regard for his own safety. Spraying its windshield with detergent and quickly wiping it clean in the hope of earning a *peso*. Smaller children meekly wiped side window with one hand, holding out their other grubby little hand expectantly. Young girls and old women could be seen weaving between the cars selling everything from hand-made woven goods to nuts, curried eggs *chicle* and cigarettes. For such people it was their only source of income. A tiny ray of hope that someone would show them pity and press a coin into their hands, before the lights turned to green and the traffic moved on. A young foreign woman passing in her limousine looked decidedly uncomfortable, as she passed a few coins to her driver who lowered his window sufficiently to press the coins into the dirty but grateful palm.

Mexico was truly a city of contrasts. Those who have' and those who have not!

Having walked for some time she sat down at the side of the road. She looked to the left and then to the right. The street was suddenly very quiet. Resting her chin in her hands she began to ponder.

She thought of Mr Twist, the poor old man who lived in the shop doorway on *Calle Lucia*. The tiny little man, his body so twisted and deformed, hence his name. No one knew his real name, in fact she had never heard him speak.

No one ever saw Mr Twist move, but occasionally he would disappear and then re-appear later in another doorway, further down the street. She had heard mention that he had rheumatoid arthritis, a chronic inflammatory disease, Enrique had told her. Although she did not fully understand she knew that it was a very painful condition and there were no painkillers for the likes of him. Poor soul.

Then there were the kids who never had a chance. What future for them? The ones who would sniff glue hoping to dull the hunger pains and to block out the misery of the streets.

Moving on slowly and dragging her feet she continued in the direction of the shelter. She saw someone huddled in a doorway, taking little notice at first because it was quite the norm in the city, particularly when the offices had closed for the day and the workers gone home. Then, those of no fixed abode would settle down for the night. Workers arriving early morning were seen to step over characters still sound asleep from the night before. Not an uncommon occurrence, most disconcerting but what could they do?

The homeless camped out everywhere, anywhere! Moved on, only later to reappear in another doorway, on another bench or behind another shelter. Well, this was the *Oficina de Ventas*, Old Ma Kensie's favourite haunt. Dolita's heart leapt momentarily but she knew by the shape and position of the body that it was not Ma Kensie. The office was obviously closed; the shutters down and the entrance dark.

With the intention of carrying on her way and ignoring the character she crossed the street to walk on the far side. Something however in her spirit troubled her. She was just about to turn back when a most horrendous noise, which sounded positively evil, startled her. A guttural screech followed by another, then another and reeling backwards a few steps she turned the corner to quickly realise that two cats were marking their territory. They were just about to embark on a ferocious fight. Dolita obviously startled them as much as they startled her. They scarpered and she turned back towards the *Oficina de Ventas*.

CHAPTER 25
BOBBY SNIFF

Moving towards the huddled mass, she soon
realized that it was Bobby Sniff. Although she
could not see his face, nor his upper body, hidden
under the mass of plastic, cardboard and shredded
paper, she recognised the trainers and the old holdall
which held all his worldly possessions. There was
no mistaking Bobby's cumbersome gigantic feet and
those odd tennis shoes, one black, the other white.
Whether by accident or design she never knew, it
didn't really matter, at least he had shoes!

"Bobby," she whispered, "Bobby, it's me, Dolita,
Bobby."

Ordinarily she would have left him, assuming him
to be sleeping, but something was nagging her. She
recalled that first meeting with Bobby Sniff when
Mikey Mean had the incident with the stolen bike.
She knew that he was close to the Molina brothers
and that he was trying desperately to get accepted
as one of the gang. It was not easy to become a gang
member but the Molina brothers were something
else. They where trouble, no doubt. They seemed to
control most of the crime in that part of town. Petty
crime that is, they weren't real gangsters, just kids
after all. But a fearsome bunch they were too,
certainly tomorrow's villains, if someone didn't take
a hold of them. An endurance test and a dare was
required and if you had proven your worth you were

still not guaranteed to be accepted into the gang. Once in however, you had to tow the line or you were soon kicked out, literally that is.

Bobby never did make the grade!

Since that first encounter at Deuno's lock-up Dolita had seen Bobby on several occasions. During his attempt to join the Molinas he indulged in body piercings and tattoo art, thinking it looked good, tough and all that! One piercing was his left ear; a nail, 4 cm in length went directly through his ear lobe protruding the other side. Grotesque, but he liked it! Making a statement, he said. Dolita thought it just proved he was potty.

Bobby was just like most of the other street kids. A reject! Abandoned, neglected, and abused a "nonperson" looking for an identity. Some of the other kids gave him the name "Bobby Sniff" because he had this annoying and persistent habit of sniffing, snorting and wiping his nose on his sleeve.

Sadly, after that first meeting at Deuno's there had been several occasions when Dolita had found Bobby sniffing glue and other unsavoury substances.

"Takes away the hunger pains," Bobby would say, and sure it did for a while at least, but only to have devastating results afterwards.

Oh yes, it numbed the hunger pains all right and all other feelings for that matter, but when the effects of the stuff wore off, it was far worse, leaving the abuser with an even greater appetite. The 'munchies' they called it! Then there were the other symptoms, such as the nausea, paranoia and cracking headaches.

234

Bobby's cycle of abuse began with sniffing shoe polish. Later, aerosols: basically anything solvent that he could get his hands on.

That temporary high, that feeling of well-being was soon gone. Feeling worse he began to look in the wrong place for answers. He looked to grass or "*porro*" as it was called, later to harder drugs. Stealing to feed the habit became his only option, as his body adjusted to the filth that he was now pumping into it, he fell deeper and deeper into addiction. Within an amazingly short time Bobby had become double-minded. The Bobby that Dolita had first met was becoming more aggressive and as for paranoia? Well, that was an understatement. He thought everyone was out to get him, seeing shadows in the shadows. She remembered the night he stumbled into the shelter and Bozo had him pinned down. Scary that must have been, and since that night he had deteriorated, quicker in fact than anyone else she had ever seen in the streets. Dolita wondered what he was now taking.

Crouching in the wretched doorway, Dolita felt a spirit of fear overshadow her as she went to shake Bobby gently. A dirty needle lay discarded by his side. A horrible gurgling sound came from beneath the plastic sheet hiding his face. Pushing it aside she gasped. Bobby's face was ghastly white, his eyes rolled to and fro and his mouth was half open. White powder and saliva dribbled and frothed down his chin. He was shivering and he seemed to have no control over his bodily functions. Dolita reeled backwards in shock and nearly broke poor Raggy

Man's leg as she tumbled on him, Raggy yelped in pain.

"*¿Qué onda? ¿Qué onda?* Oh Raggy Man, what has Bobby done now? What do I do? Is he dead? No he's not dead, stupid me, can't be 'cos he's making those horrible noises."

For what seemed like an eternity and now gripped by fear Dolita continued to have a conversation with herself and Raggy who was sitting in the opposite corner of the doorway, licking his wound.

"That hurt!" but he knew Dolita was too involved with another situation to bother about him and his sore leg.

Her mind was working overtime. Should she go for help? Was there time? Was Bobby dying? She felt sure he was!

Dolita looked around and the street was empty and disturbingly quiet. Strange the street was never empty. Where was help when you needed it? She thought of Bobby dying alone. It did not bear thinking about. She could not leave her friend and she felt the courage to move forward and take his hand. It felt cold. Her head whirling, she hoped Bobby was just having a bad day. Maybe he was not dying at all and would be all right if he slept it off. I don't think so! Well possibly a shock. Yes, a shock. She would shock him out of it. That's it! Slap him about the face a few times. Shock him out of it. That would do wouldn't it?

She shook him, she slapped him, she screamed at him. All to no avail. Her heart cried out. Would somebody please help her? Would somebody please

236

help her friend Bobby? She slumped back and wanted to cry, but taking a deep breath fought back the tears. She must be tough. Street Kids don't cry.

"Oh why? Oh why? Oh why?" The anguish welled up inside her.

Suddenly she recalled the dream. Which dream, I hear you asking? Dolita had many dreams.

Yes! Remember the one where she found herself in Heavenly places.

That beautiful setting in her dreams.

Remember, when she saw all the children and how happy they were, the older guy trailing behind in the group who knew her name. He had looked just like Bobby. Well sort of a bit different but an uncanny resemblance. She was reminded of that look of peace in his eyes, how strange, how very odd. Was it some sort of premonition?

If so she suddenly felt better. If Bobby died was he going to a better place? Raggy barked and startled her, back in the land of reality her eyes met with Bobby's. Momentarily he seemed aware of her and he smiled, a sort of crooked, half-smile, she knew it was going to be OK. Fixing his gaze on something beyond her, as though there was someone behind her, he found the strength to speak. Dolita neither understood nor dare turn around. Was Bobby talking in English? But how? When did Bobby learn English? she puzzled.

Perhaps she was not meant to understand, it was certainly a foreign language. Whatever the case she watched as the muscles in his face relaxed. The tension and the emptiness left his eyes, which began to sparkle, as he whispered the name Jesus. With a last surge of energy he squeezed her hand, then Bobby was gone. He closed his eyes and she knew he was gone.

Wiping away the few salty teardrops from her cheeks with the sleeves of her sweater, the one she had found at the basura. She was determined not to cry, Street Kids don't cry! She turned round but no one was there. Raggy made enough noise in the street to gain the attention of a passer-by. As soon as they arrived, she slipped away, only to hear that three days later Bobby Sniff was put to rest. Father Jose took the ceremony.

CHAPTER 26
NAVIDAD

Since that horrible event Dolita had barely left the shelter and memories of Bobby's death overshadowed her. A few days before Christmas and evidence of the festivities were beginning to spring up everywhere. In Mexico the Christmas season continued until the eve of January 6, ending with *El Dia de Reyes* known to the English as the Three Kings Day. Processions and celebrations called *posadas* would echo, as a reminder, the arrival in Bethlehem of the Three Wise Men bearing gifts for Baby Jesus. Children throughout Mexico would be anxiously waiting to find toys and gifts left by the Reyes. It has always been customary in some regions to leave children's shoes in the windows so that the Reyes or Magi (another name for them) would know at which house to stop.

Having the courage to finally leave the shelter, she left alone refusing to allow Manolo and Angelina to accompany her.

"Why do you want to be on your own?" asked Angelina concerned about what appeared to be Dolita's depressive state of mind.

"Just do!" snapped Dolita and with a backward glance strolled on. She walked towards the *Zócalo* otherwise known as the *Plaza de la Constitution*. In the evening it would be ablaze with a sea of colourful lights, a reminder of that momentous evening in September when there had been the *El Grito* cry. Dolita rarely went out during the evening on her own, and she was now a considerable distance from the safety of the shelter.

"What is Christmas all about?" thought Dolita, as she wandered through the streets. The date was December 16, the beginning of the festivities. Nine consecutive days of candlelight *posadas* centred very much around children, who were often decked out in colourful handmade costumes and carrying brightly coloured, decorated baculos (walking sticks) and *faroles* (paper lanterns).

The purpose behind the *posadas* was originally an active way of teaching the children about the story and birth of the Baby Jesus. Sadly, much of the meaning had been lost with more emphasis on the merrymaking, the ruthless smashing of piñatas and a mad scramble for the fruits and sweets that the piñatas contained.

Decorated Christmas trees and nativity scenes with clay figures were set up in many of the homes and although Dolita rarely went into a "real home" (other than Beeky's perhaps) she had on occasions caught glimpses through the windows of some of the smaller houses as she passed by. The larger houses certainly could not be seen, well hidden behind the high perimeter walls and obtrusive security fences. Dolita wandered for hours, amazingly she managed to sneak into the foyer of one of the grand hotels before being discovered by a brusque security guard and being thrown out. How she sneaked in was a daring feat for a street kid but something that she was determined to try at least once.

240

Hiding behind the luggage trolley and the entourage of guests all clamouring to get through the swing doors, she managed to squeeze between them, and remarkably managed to get as far as the entrance to the first restaurant.

Raggy Man nestled snugly under her arm knew something precarious was going on and kept exceedingly still, not to mention quiet. Dolita could hear talk of preparations for an exotic feast on *Noche Buena* - roast suckling pig, turkey, ham and hot fruit punch. The wild greens in mole sauce sounded disgusting!

"Oh, Raggy Man. I don't fancy the mole sauce but I sure would like a piece of that turkey," she whispered.

"Raspberry truffle, Mmmm... yummy... Sounds good. I wonder what it is." Before she heard another word she was being escorted rather roughly out of the building having being discovered.

What a commotion, she was only a kid after all. Why had she created so much attention. Don't think they like us Raggy she whispered picking herself up and examining her bruised and scuffed knees, after her little body had scraped the pavement.

Silently walking away from the hotel Dolita recalled that the beggar woman Old Ma Kensie had told her that Christmas Eve was always rounded off with the opening of presents for the children. Uhm…! Ma Kensie, how she missed her old friend. Had she too died in a doorway like Bobby Sniff? To be taken away and become just another stastistic. Oh Ma Kensie, Ma Kensie, Ma Kensie! Where are you? And what about Pablo Molina, the friendship that never was…?

Slumping in a doorway, Raggy Man by her side, the sadness of the streets overwhelmed her. She didn't know how long it had been since she had eaten, the hunger pains becoming a reality in a way she had never known before.

"*¡Tengo hambre,* Raggy! *¡Tengo hambre!*"

A Mexican family crossed the street below her and their two young children chattered gleefully as they tossed sunflower seeds to a few wandering pigeons. Their little girl carried a rag doll, but not nearly as beautiful as the doll Charlotte had given her. A faint but very weak smile dawned on Dolita's face. Charlotte… she liked Charlotte.

A young Indian girl passed by, her three children trailing behind, carrying all their worldly belongings in green plastic bags. A boy ran to catch up with them holding an enormous drum base, it looked heavy, the poor little mite could barely see over the top of it. The church bells rang out in the distance as a tall skinny boy picked up a dirty plastic cup that had the dregs of a cappuccino, presumably purchased from a nearby kiosk or open-air bar and discarded by a punter. He slurped the remaining contents, grimaced and spat them out. Then burying his head in a nearby trash-can he surfaced with several items after he had combed it thoroughly for foodstuffs. He looked a little older than Roberto, in fact he bore much resemblance to him, the likeness was uncanny. He ate what looked like the remains of an *enchilada* ravenously. Dolita studied them all quietly; living in the same city but how different their lives must be. She reached over and pulled Raggy Man to her side, squeezing him with all the love she could muster.

"So indeed what is Christmas all about?" she asked Raggy Man. I suppose that depends on who is asking the question! Her mind drifted again to Pablo Molina. She thought of Bobby Sniff. If only…? Ma Kensie and Alejandro, all gone. Dolita remembered Alejandro's parting words to her. He begged her to take up the place he had reserved in one of the *Hogares de Niños*, but, in spite of the pain and misery of the streets, they were still her home. The streets were still in her veins, in her blood. How could she ever leave her friends in the shelter, they would all have to come too! Unless…? She thought deeply, unless…? What if…?

Dolita unravelled a piece of torn linen earlier wrapped around her middle and tied neatly behind her back. As it unfolded the vibrant stripes of the doll's clothing could be seen: the precious *muñeca* that Charlotte had given her. The corners of her mouth curled as she smiled half-heartedly. That feeling of rejection, self-blame. "Did I do something wrong, Raggy? Was it my fault? Why does everyone leave me?"

* * *

In spite of the love she felt for Raggy she felt a huge chasm of loneliness. Knowing that she must not give up hope, she studied the doll, lovingly squeezed Raggy and whispered, "Oh please, please, come back Charlotte."

Tears fell from her cheeks; she snivelled and wiped them away.

'Street kids don't cry'.

Then with a deep breath and exhorting every tiny bit of energy in her weary body, she screamed at the top of her voice.

"Will somebody please help me find my mum!"

CHAPTER 27
THE END OR A NEW BEGINNING?

So what is Christmas all about?" asked Enrie Molina, his deferred parole notice in his hand.

"For me, this year, freedom!" answered his cellmate smiling, thinking of a typical day in those miserable surroundings; he hardly dared believe this Christmas represented freedom. So many days spent in confinement, in that small dark miserable room. Its solid door and tiny windows restricting any light, not being able to see what lurked on the other side! Sound was everything. The footsteps on the landing, the high-pitched clanking of the warden's keys and sometimes the insane shouting of the other prisoners. The constant smell of urine and sweat, even fear had a smell.

The bolts being released on the doors, the morning cry, "Slop out".

Was it Tuesday or Wednesday? Who knows, who cares? Thank God another day nearer to release, yet it seemed an eternity away.

The voice in the distance, "Landing 4, *desayuno*." The thought of the silent walk down the corridor for a cold mug of weak coffee and a cob of stale bread.

"Why did I bother?"

Lost in his memories he looked into Molina's eyes. Poor bloke, for him there was no freedom this

Christmas, another year to wait, yet, we reap what we sow, he was paying the price. For the other lads, mundane work, soul-destroying, repetitive. If they wanted a piece of *chicle* or perhaps sugar in their coffee, they would have to work. No work, no perks. He remembered Enrie's words when he came out of solitary and was put in a cell with him, "Keep your head down, boy. Don't upset anyone and most of all me! You don't know what these guys are in here for, burglary, arson, drug trafficking, rape or murder. The most angelic face can hide the most vicious of natures. Stay on guard and just do your time quietly."

It was the best advice anyone could ever have given him.

Dinner, oh deep joy! The call for dinner and his last meal in that God-forsaken place: some sloppy beans and something vaguely resembling meat.

A fight broke out in the corner and the inmates were quickly escorted back to their cells.

Christmas this year represented Freedom for someone.

* * *

It was his last night and he didn't sleep. He was almost afraid to sleep in case it all turned out to be just a dream. He lay on his bunk, his eyes a glaze, staring but seeing nothing, thinking but his head empty. No! he dare not sleep, he dare not think. He was waiting, waiting for daybreak. The hours passed slowly. That last night seemed to last forever and then suddenly as if he had missed something, a segment of time, there he was.

He stood outside the prison gates, gulping fresh air, awash in the sun. Wearing dark glasses, a black and white checked bandana and jeans he looked positively *guapo*. Brown skin, a tattoo on his upper arm, a fake diamond stud in his right ear. How long he had yearned to be free, nine years of life wasted. The feelings rose up inside him. He was young enough to start his life again, and this he was determined to do. He would close the doors on the past and as he walked away from those dark, angry-looking walls, which housed so many secrets, he felt re-born.

The pain of the days inside quickly fading, the memories would stay with him forever.

Once bitter and angry, convicted of a crime he didn't commit. Yes, he dealt a little coke here and there, but murder no, definitely not! He was in the wrong place at the wrong time, framed for something he didn't do. His desire for vengeance had gone, it was in God's hands now. Believing everyone would be accountable to their maker one day, he just wanted to focus on the future.

It was a most exhilarating feeling. Yes, he felt reborn.

With virtually no belongings, what little he had in a torn brown paper bag, certainly no money, the future was daunting.

Murmuring to himself and thanking God for Nicky and Enrie, the guys who had befriended him inside, he walked on.

Shame about Enrie's parole. Nicky had been out for the past couple of months but Enrie Molina's had been put off again. The three of them had forged quite a relationship, well you do sharing a tiny four by three metre cell for several years!

He waited hesitantly, enjoying the taste of freedom and a smile of relief crossed his face as he saw the friendly old guy coming round the corner in a rusty, clapped out jeep, tooting his horn.

"Jump in mate," he shouted. His eyes dazzling and grinning from ear to ear, he threw open the passenger door which was so old and rotten it creaked painfully and very nearly came off its hinges.

"What's the plan?" asked Nicky.

"No plan," chortled his mate. "Just one day at a time but need to make some money fast, enough to pay my air fare to Madrid."

"Sounds like a plan to me. What's that you have there?" he asked, pointing to a piece of paper that had just fallen out of his mate's torn pocket when he had clambered in.

"Wouldn't be a 50-dollar note, by any chance would it?" he squawked with laughter and reached down scooping up the paper and handing it to his mate.

"Yeah, I wish! Too good to be true," he unraveled the note and read the name Helga, then the number, scribbled but legible. He smiled and placed it safely back into his trouser pocket.

"What have you been doing this last couple of months?" he asked Nicky.

"Oh this and that."

"Good to be out, eh!"

"Yeah, sure is pal! Juan there's a deal…"

"Don't even think about it, don't even mention it. I'm going straight."

"Now come on dude, here's the deal………"

"No man, I'm not rolling. I wouldn't trade the peace that I have in my heart for anything this crazy world could offer."

Nick looked at Juan curiously.

"What you on pal? *¿Qué onda? ¿Qué onda?* What 'appened to you? Sounds a bit profound for you."

"Nick, all that this world offers are diamonds made of dust. I'm richer now than gold could ever make me," said Juan smiling. Nick's jaw dropped, staring at Juan, he nearly collided with a tree which seemed to loom up from nowhere. Swerving to regain control of his jeep he leaned forward precariously pressing his forehead against the windscreen.

"You're different dude, what 'appened to you? 'Av you 'ad one of those God experiences or something?"

Juan smirked, "I'll tell you over a nice cool beer but do you wanna know what I'm gonna do with my life now? I've business in Madrid and then I'm back to Mexico D.F.: I'm gonna find my kid."

"What kid? I didn't know you 'ad a kid. You kept that one quiet."

"Yeah well! I once met a girl, the most beautiful thing you ever did see. I didn't treat her real good, and I'm not proud of it. She was pregnant when I got banged up. Never did see her again.

Come to think of it don't know whether it's a boy or a girl but the kid should be about nine years old now. Yeah, I've got business in Madrid then I'm gonna find my kid."

The car drove on.

* * *

Back at the shelter, "It's Christmas," mumbled Roberto. "We should go to church." The others looked at him in amazement.

"¡Vale! ¡Vale!" said Roberto taking his cap off his head and then having thought better of it, replacing it.

"OK. Well let's have a song at least," said Roberto.

"What's got into you?" asked Manolo. "Shouldn't you be sleeping?"

"Yeah," said Angelina, "come on Hugh give us a song."

"Don't feel like singing, I'm worried about Dolita!"

"Where is she anyway? I'm going to look for her," said Enrique. "She's been gone too long on her own."

Before they had chance to move a muscle, Father Jose peered round the shelter wall.

"Who's he?" mumbled Roberto, startled by his appearance.

"Well, you are the one who mentioned church, seems like church has come to you," said Manolo, laughing heartily.

"Ah, this is Father Jose," said Enrique, introducing him as though they were old friends.

"Pepi, to you," exclaimed the Father, who wore black slacks, black shirt and a white dog collar.

"My friends call me Pepi," he said, with a cheeky grin.

"Who said we'll be friends?" asked Mikey sarcastically, studying the stranger.

Father Jose smiled and nodded.

"We met at the Crisis Centre," said Enrique. "He is *chido* man," he exclaimed. "He's the one who took Bobby Sniff's funeral. Everyone loves him, he's a bit like a re-cycled teenager."

"Right, good stuff," said Mikey, not impressed at all, but he shook hands with the guy anyway.

* * *

"Want an avocado?" asked Mikey, "Pepi's the name, you say!"

"Thanks, but no thanks," replied Pepi. "Just passing and thought I'd call and check out the shelter. Heard from Enrique there were about fifteen of you hanging about here. One or two youngsters as well."

"Yeah, and before you ask, they won't go."

"Go where?" asked Pepi in answer to Mikey's curt remark.

"No *Hogares de Niños* and all that stuff. If you mean Dolita, Angelina and Manolo, they won't go. The streets are in their blood, man and they won't leave the other *chavos*. Us *chavos*, we stick together, you know!"

"Sure, quite understand," said Pepi raising his chin and his eyebrows simultaneously and nodding his head. "I wanted to ask you about the kids who live in the sewers," said Pepi.

"What about them?" asked Mikey.

"Well do you know any of them?"

"No," said Mikey "and I don't want to. My advice is don't go snooping around those sewers. Most of those kids down there are *loco*, seriously *loco*. If you've any sense, keep away."

Enrique looked concerned, very concerned. "Don't get any of your fancy ideas now, Father Pepi" said Enrique. "Mikey is right about this one, keep away. You can't help them."

Suddenly, Raggy's bark could be heard in the distance and they all relaxed. Dolita was on her way home; a sigh of relief on everyone's faces. Angelina rushed out to meet her, outstretched arms engulfing her in a huge bear hug. Enrique followed, taking hold of the young Dolita and scooping her up, just as he had done that day when he had returned to find her hiding in the clump of bushes outside the Grand Hotel. "Dolita, Dolita," he said, "don't frighten us like that, we were all so worried!"

"*¡Tengo hambre!*" she whimpered, "*¡Tengo hambre!*"

"Well then, we'll try and find you some food, *mi pequena botón de oro !*"

This was one occasion when she didn't mind Enrique's playful pet name, in fact she felt overwhelmed, as Mikey, Roberto and the others all greeted her profusely. Realising how the other kids cared for her, she suddenly felt, all "loved up". She had a family after all. This was her family!

"Hi, said the stranger. "Father Jose to some, Pepi to you" he said with a twinkle in his eye. Dolita liked him, he had a kind face, and something about him... yes she liked him."
"Well, I must be off" said Pepi. "Nice to meet you all, "*Hasta luego*"..... he hesitated. "Oh, forgot to mention, I was at the Crisis Centre yesterday and they said to tell you....remember that old beggar woman that you were all so fond of...Kerry, Kenny or someone, forgot the name."

"Kensie, said Roberto mumbling."

"Yeah, that's the one. She turned up yesterday."

Dolita's head spun round so fast it nearly fell off her shoulders. "*Eh*! What did you say?"

"That woman, Old Ma Kensie, turned up yesterday. Been missing for ages Daveed told me, thought she was dead or something."

Dolita's jaw dropped. Ma Kensie, Old Ma Kensie had turned up. Today was a good day after all!

Hence my story ends and now you have met the "Street Kids" or Chavos as they are often called.
I trust you are beginning to love Dolita as much as I do.

Look out for Book 2 and more stories of life on the streets down town Mexico D.F.

Oh! and............. Will Dolita find her mum?

The story teller.

Mole Sauce

Mole is part of traditional Mexican cuisine and the dark brown sauce is typically served on special occasions with turkey, since it is time consuming to prepare. It actually contains 40 ingredients, here are just a few:

- Mulato chilli
- Tomato
- Toasted sesame seeds
- Sugar
- Chocolate

- Fried torilla
- Garlic
- Almonds
- Raisins
- Cinnamon

The real recipe for this delicious gravy is quite complex, but here is a simplified version for you to try at home with Mum!

1) Roast the tomatoes until soft and place in a bowl.
2) Toast the sesame seeds, stirring constantly, until golden. Add to the tomatoes.
3) Tear the chillies into pieces and fry in oil until inside changes to a lighter colour (about 30 secs). Place in an empty bowl. Cover with hot tap water and keep submerged. Stand for 30 mins.
4) Fry the garlic and almonds, stirring regularly. Place with tomatoes and sesame seeds.

5) Heat raisins in a pan until they are puffed and browned, (30 secs). Add to the tomatoes.

6) Use tongs to transfer chillies to a blender. Taste the soaking liquid, and if not bitter, measure a few cups into the blender. (If bitter, use water). Blend to a smooth puree, pour back into the bowl.

7) Scrape the tomato mixture into the blender. Add 1-cup water, cinnamon, cloves and chocolate. Blend to a smooth puree, pour back into bowl.

8) Pour chilli puree into pan with oil. Stir constantly until the mixture has darkened and thickened to the consistency of tomato paste, (10-15 mins).
Add the tomato puree and continue stirring until once again thickened, (another 5-10 mins).

9) Add 6 cups water to the pan and simmer for 45 mins. Taste and season with salt and sugar.

Serving suggestion: Sear a turkey breast, cover with mole, and cook at 325°F for about 40 minutes.

GLOSARIO ESPAÑOL-INGLÉS/ SPANISH-ENGLISH GLOSSARY

A.F.I. (Agencia Federal de Investigaciones) - F.B.I. of Mexico

Autobús *(m)* - bus

Basura *(f)* - refuse, rubbish or trash

Botón de oro *(m)* - buttercup (flower)

Burrito *(m)* - flour tortilla wrapped around a savoury filling such as meat, salsa and cheese

¡Cállate! - shut up!

Calle *(f)* - street, lane or alley

Casita *(f)* - a small house, cottage

Chapulín/es *(Méx) (m/pl)* - fried grasshopper(s)

Chapusero *(m)* - a cheater (usually in games)

Chavo/a *(colloq) (m/f)* - boy/girl

Chayote *(m)* - a mirliton; pale green vegetable found in Mexico, that can be eaten raw or cooked

Chicle *(m)* - chewing gum

Chico/a *(m/f)* - boy/girl

¡Chido! *(Méx. colloq)* - cool!

Chiquito/a *(m/f)* - little or tiny one, usually used to describe a baby

Chorizo *(m)* - highly seasoned pork sausage

Cochino *(m)* - pig; filthy thing *(colloq.)*

Conejo *(m)* - rabbit

Cucaracha *(f)* - cockroach

Desayuno *(m)* - breakfast

Dia de Independencia - Independence Day

Director/a *(m/f)* - manager, chief, head of department

Distrito Federal *(m)* - Mexico City

Donde - where

¿Dónde? - where?/from what place? (question)

El Grito - Mexico's Day of Independence

Enchilada *(Méx) (f)* - rolled up tortilla dipped in sauce, baked or fried

Escuincle/a *(Méx) (m/f)* - scruffy little urchin / kid

Fútbol *(m)* - football

Gringo/a *(m/f)* - a visitor or foreigner to Latin America sometimes used in a derogatory way

Guacamole *(m)* - mashed avocados mixed with onion, chilli, lemon and tomato

Guapo/a - goodlooking

Güero/a *(Méx) (m/f)* - a term used to describe a blonde haired person

Hasta *(abbrev.)* - short for *Hasta luego*

Hogar de Niños *(m)* - a children's home

Hombre *(m)* - man

Huevo *(m)* - egg

Jamón *(m)* - ham

Las Posadas - processions during the days building up toChristmas Eve in Mexico, commemorating the events from Nazareth to Bethlehem

Loco/a *(m/f)* - crazy, mad

Mariachi *(m)* - a band of usually 11 men in fancy costumes with a variety of musical instruments

Mariposa *(f)* - butterfly

Médico/a *(m/f)* - doctor

Mermelada de frambuesa *(f)* - raspberry jam

Mujer *(f)* - Woman

Muñeca *(f)* - doll

Navidad *(f)* - Christmas

Necio - silly, foolish

Noche Buena *(f)* - Christmas Eve
Oficina de la Procuraduría *(f)* - Social Services
Oficina de Información y Turismo *(f)* -
Information/Tourist Office
Oficina de Ventas *(f)* - Sales Office
Padrote *(Méx) (m)* - pimp
Pequeño - little, small
Peso *(m)* - unit of currency
Piñata *(f)* - container hung up during festivities
and hit with a stick to release sweets
Plaza *(f)* - a square in a town or village
Policía *(f)* - police
Porque - because
¿Por qué? - why?
Promotor/a *(m/f)* - instigator, leader
Pueblo/s *(m/pl)* - village(s)
Queso *(m)* - cheese
Rambla *(f)* - dry river bed
Rápido - rapid, swift, quickly
Rata/s *(f/pl)* - rat(s)
Sueño *(m)* - a dream
Tequila *(f)* - liqueur made from plant extract
(agave)
Zócalo *(Méx) (m)* - main plaza or city square

Expresiones/Expressions

¡Conocerlo es amarlo! - knowing it is loving it!
Es un chiste - it's a joke
¿Hablas (from *hablar*) español? - do you speak Spanish?
Hasta luego - see you later
Lo siento - I'm sorry
¡Mira! - look!
Mucha suerte - good luck
¡Muy elegante! - very smart/elegant!
¡No problema! - no problem!
Por avión - by air or plane
¡Qué chido! - how cool!
¡Qué lindo! - how beautiful/lovely!
¡Qué mango! *(Méx. colloq)*- he's gorgeous!
¡Qué rico! - delicious!
Qué será, será - whatever wil be, will be
Suficiente para sobrevivir - enough to survive
Tengo (from *tener*) hambre - I'm hungry
Tengo (from *tener*) sed - I'm thirsty
¿Qué onda? *(colloq)* - what's new? what happened?
Vale - ok
¡Vamos a ver! - let's go and see!
¡Viva México! - long live Mexico!

Notas Gramáticas / Grammar Notes

1) Spanish nouns always take a gender, which is either masculine or femenine. The lower cases *(m)* and *(f)* indicate which. *(m/f)* indicates the noun adopts either, depending on the gender of the object it refers to.
2) Nouns are generally written in their masculine; singular form, in a glossary
3) Phrases containing verbs indicate the infinitive in brackets e.g. "Tengo (from *tener*) hambre"
4) Latin American Spanish occasionally differs from Iberian Spanish, *(Méx)* indicates the term is specfic to Mexico
5) *(Colloq)* implies a colloquial or slang term
6) *(Abbrev.)* indicates an abbreviated form of the word/expression

STREET KiD CODE

Rule 1: If you have it, share it!

Rule 2: If a kid's in trouble, be there!

Rule 3: If a kid wants to talk, listen.

Rule 4: If you make a promise, keep it.

Rule 5: If he confides in you, don't betray him."

Rule 6: Never mock, ridicule or be cruel to a street kid."

Rule 7: Treat other kids the way you would like them to treat you.

Rule 8: Respect one another, treating everyone as equal.
No lesser
Survival's the game.